零失敗、好上手
HOLD 住全場贏下會話不是夢，
就是現在，馬上開口說！

How to use 使用說明

1

模擬多樣的會話情境

想自然而然地在日常生活
中使用英語會話,但卻不
知道各種情境的講法?別
擔心,本書分為7大項主
題,各主題中又包含了各
式各樣的生活情境,全書
共51種情境講法,你想
到的、沒想到的我們都包
了,絕對讓你能準確地使
用這些句子,侃侃而談!

2

問句答句分別設區不混亂

本書貼心地分設「你可以這
樣問」的問句區塊及「你可
以這樣說」的答句區塊,你
再也不會在要發問或回答時
因為翻半天找不到適合會話
句而感到驚慌,問句、答句
分區讓你輕鬆問、順利答!

Chapter 01 飲食

「家裡用餐」

你可以這樣問

What do you want for breakfast? ◀ Track 001

你早餐想吃什麼?
▶ How about ham and eggs for breakfast?
早餐吃火腿和蛋如何?
▶ Do you want a peanut butter sandwich for breakfast?
你想要來一份花生醬三明治當早餐嗎?

Where's my morning paper? ◀ Track 002

我的早報呢?

morning paper
的相反是
evening paper
「晚報」。

你可以這樣說

Your breakfast is on the dining ◀ Track 003
table.

你的早餐在餐桌上。
▶ I made some cereal for breakfast.
我準備了些麥片當早餐。
▶ Breakfast will be ready in three minutes.
早餐再三分鐘就好了。

I want to have some bread and ◀ Track
butter for breakfast.

我想吃麵包加奶油當早餐。
▶ Can I have something hot to drink?
我可以喝些熱的東西嗎?

012

3

豐富的實用例句補充

語言是活的,同樣一件事情絕對不止一種
講法。本書除了教你英語會話之外,也希
望你能活用補充例句將對話敘述變得更加
多采多姿,不知不覺中不只記起了更多實
用用法,也將英語用得更道地了!

4

重點單字註解說明

使用灰色小框框來說明會話句子中的單字,確保你能讀懂會話句中的各個單字,並能根據會話情境來更換所需單字,使你的英語會話知識不只變得更深入,還能變得更加寬廣!

Could you make me a cup of hot chocolate?
你可以幫我弄杯熱可可嗎?

Do we still have some orange juice in the fridge?
我們冰箱裡還有柳橙汁嗎?

> fridge 是 refrigerator 冰箱 的簡稱。

don't have time for breakfast. ◀ Track 005
沒時間吃早餐了。

> I can only take a few bites before I run.
> 我只能吃幾口就得出門了。

> I have to skip breakfast.
> 我今天不吃早餐了。

> skip 有「略過」的意思,在這裡就是表示「不吃早餐了」

> I'll just have a cup of coffee. 我喝杯咖啡就好。

like to have Chinese-style breakfast. ◀ Track 006
我喜歡吃中式的早餐。

> American breakfast is my favorite.
> 美式早餐是我的最愛。

> 美式早餐除了麵包、可頌以外,還有培根、炒蛋等熱食及咖啡、牛奶、果汁等選擇。

My wife makes breakfast for me every day. ◀ Track 007
我太太每天幫我準備早餐。

> We always have breakfast in a hurry.
> 我們總是匆忙地吃早餐。

> I insist that the kids must have breakfast before they go to school.
> 我堅持孩子們上學前一定要吃早餐。

> Breakfast is the most important meal of the day.
> 早餐是一天中最重要的一餐。

5

外籍講師專業發音MP3

本書請來外籍講師按各例句示範專業發音,在邊聽邊唸的同時,不只會話力增加,聽力也能大幅增進!另外,特別設計成一句一音檔,好找不費時!

Special 臨時好用150句

「坐車、開車出門,出發前一定要知道」

① We're stuck in the traffic.
我們塞在車陣中了。

② Is there a parking lot around here?
這附近有停車場嗎?

③ I can't start the engine.
我無法發動引擎。

④ Could you check the brakes for me?
請你幫我檢查一下煞車好嗎?

⑤ I think there's something wrong with the transmission.
我覺得車子的變速箱有問題。

⑥ I'm almost out of gas.
車子快要沒油了。

⑦ I got a ticket for speeding.
我收到一張超速罰單。

6

超值附錄:臨時好用150句

本書最後部分為你統整出各種情況中,在出發前臨時記起會超級實用的150句例句,超棒設計,即使再慌忙的情況都能成功用這些例句HOLD住全場!

Preface 作者序

所謂的「語言」就是一種與不同文化背景的人溝通交流的工具，既然是溝通交流，「聽、讀、寫」固然重要，「說」也是不可或缺的一環，但這也是大部分人最擔心的地方，以致於常有「明明學習很久的英文、有一定基礎，卻仍不敢開口說」的窘境。這本書就是以「想要改變這種狀況」的想法下去設計，用實用又精準的句子讓讀者熟記後不只能說得好、還可以說得道地！

本書將生活中會遇到的各種狀況分作7大類，涵蓋居家生活常用高頻率會話；自我介紹時必學的內外表達會話；能和人打成一片的興趣與嗜好會話；遭遇緊急狀況時得說的臨場會話；幫助快速適應環境的學校職場會話；跟上潮流趨勢必知的深度會話；以及從行程安排到結束返家都用得到的旅遊會話，不管是表達自己還是與他人聊天，甚至到觀光會話都詳細收錄，貼心替你考慮到所有可能會用到的句子，當然也少不了補充例句及單字，不只是單純地死背會話，還能從此將句子變成活用句，舉一反三才實用！

另外，本書將各情境內的會話再細分為「問句」與「敘述句」兩大類，為的就是讓你可以更快速地查找到當下需要的會話句－想開口詢

問他人時就從問句下手查找；想回答別人的問題時便從敘述句裡面挑選合適的答覆，如此使用會話，才能不只正確，更是快速有效率！

最後，考量到大家有臨時外出旅行，沒時間做好會話準備的狀況，所以本書也把出發前臨時會用到的必學句子彙整起來，有需求時快速翻閱查找，用最短的時間，解決最多的問題，即便臨時抱佛腳也抱得緊、抱得牢！

本書的主旨，是希望幫讀者想到全方位的使用情境，並且提供平易近人又實用的句子，期盼用簡單好上手的內容，讓讀者們可以毫無畏懼地說出來，畢竟要能說出口，才會有人與人間的溝通交流，也才會進一步地有「使用語言」的意義！

張瑩安

Contents 目錄

Part 1
讓你快意人生的**居家生活會話**

Part 2
讓你表達自我的**外表內在講法**

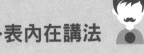

Part 3
讓你輕鬆閒聊的**興趣嗜好會話**

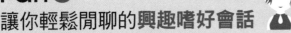

Part 4
讓你不用驚慌的**緊急狀況講法**

What can we do when an earthquake happens?

Part5
讓你快速融入的**學校職場會話**

What's your favorite subject?

Part6
讓你跟上潮流的**現代新知講法**

Part 7
讓你沒有壓力的旅遊度假會話

We're stuck in the traffic.

Special
貼心嚴選──出發前必學情境

Part 1

讓你快意人生的
居家生活會話

「家裡用餐」

你可以這樣問

💬 **What do you want for breakfast?** ◀ *Track 001*

你早餐想吃什麼？

▶ How about ham and eggs for breakfast?
早餐吃火腿和蛋如何？

▶ Do you want a peanut butter sandwich for breakfast?
你想要來一份花生醬三明治當早餐嗎？

• •

morning paper
的相反是
evening paper
「晚報」。

💬 **Where's my morning paper?** ◀ *Track 002*

我的早報呢？

• •

你可以這樣說

💬 **Your breakfast is on the dining** ◀ *Track 003*
table.

你的早餐在餐桌上。

▶ I made some cereal for breakfast.
我準備了些麥片當早餐。

▶ Breakfast will be ready in three minutes.
早餐再三分鐘就好了。

• •

💬 **I want to have some bread and** ◀ *Track 004*
butter for breakfast.

我想吃麵包加奶油當早餐。

▶ Can I have something hot to drink?
我可以喝些熱的東西嗎？

▶ Could you make me a cup of hot chocolate?
你可以幫我弄杯熱可可嗎？

▶ Do we still have some orange juice in the fridge?
我們冰箱裡還有柳橙汁嗎？

> fridge 是 refrigerator 冰箱 的簡稱。

I don't have time for breakfast. ◀ *Track 005*
我沒時間吃早餐了。

▶ I can only take a few bites before I run.
我只能吃幾口就得出門了。

▶ I have to skip breakfast.
我今天不吃早餐了。

▶ I'll just have a cup of coffee. 我喝杯咖啡就好。

> skip 有「略過」的意思，在這裡就是表示「不吃早餐了」。

I like to have Chinese-style breakfast. ◀ *Track 006*
我喜歡吃中式的早餐。

▶ American breakfast is my favorite.
美式早餐是我的最愛。

> 美式早餐除了麵包、可頌以外，還有培根、炒蛋等熱食及咖啡、牛奶、果汁等選擇。

My wife makes breakfast for me every day. ◀ *Track 007*
我太太每天幫我準備早餐。

▶ We always have breakfast in a hurry.
我們總是匆忙地吃早餐。

▶ I insist that the kids must have breakfast before they go to school.
我堅持孩子們上學前一定要吃早餐。

▶ Breakfast is the most important meal of the day.
早餐是一天中最重要的一餐。

I need to buy cornflakes for breakfast.

Track 008

我需要買早餐的玉米片了。

▶ We have run out of cereal and milk.
麥片和牛奶已經沒有了。

▶ Please buy some toast on your way home this evening.
請你今天晚上回家時順便買些吐司。

「外食用餐」

你可以這樣問

When are the opening hours?

Track 009

請問營業時間是？

「營業時間」可使用 service hours 或 trading hours。

▶ Is it easy to find a parking space around there?
在那附近停車方便嗎？

▶ Is it convenient to drive there?
那裡開車過去方便嗎？

parking lot 停車場；parking space 停車位；parking fee 停車費

▶ Which is the nearest MRT station?
離那裡最近的捷運站是哪一站？

For here or to go?

Track 010

請問要內用還是外帶？

▶ Please wait over there. 請你在那邊稍等。

▶ Here's your receipt. 這是您的收據。

Where can I get some ketchup? 🔊 Track 011

請問蕃茄醬要在哪裡拿？

▶ How many packs do you need? 你需要幾包？
▶ Can I have some more black pepper?
我可以再要一些黑胡椒嗎？

Is the seat taken? 🔊 Track 012

這位子有人坐嗎？

▶ Do you still need the newspaper?
請問你還需要這份報紙嗎？

若要表示座位已
有人坐，可用
occupied。

Would you prefer a smoking or a non-smoking area? 🔊 Track 013

請問需要吸菸區或非吸菸區？

▶ The table is reserved. 這桌有人訂位了。
▶ Would you prefer an indoor or an outdoor area?
請問需要室內或室外的位置？
▶ I'm afraid you might need to wait for few minutes.
恐怕你要等個幾分鐘。

appetizer 開胃
菜；main course
主餐；side dish
附餐

May I take your order? 🔊 Track 014

我可以為您點餐了嗎？

▶ How would you like your steak?
您的牛排需要幾分熟？
▶ What else do you need?
你還需要些什麼？

well done 全熟；
well medium 七
分熟；medium
五分熟；rare 三
分熟

scrambled egg
炒蛋；boiled egg
水煮蛋；sunny-
side up egg
荷包蛋

What do you recommend?

Track 015

你有任何推薦的餐點嗎？

▶ What's today's special? 今日特餐是什麼？

▶ The banana split is one of our hot sale items.
香蕉船是本店的人氣商品之一。

best selling
最暢銷

▶ No, thanks. I'm allergic to shrimp.
不，謝謝。我對蝦子過敏。

Do you have a Chinese menu?

Track 016

請問有中文的菜單嗎？

▶ Do you have a vegetarian menu?
請問有素食菜單嗎？

▶ Where's the beverage list? 飲料單在哪裡？

你可以這樣說

I need something low fat and low caffeine.

Track 017

我需要低脂和低咖啡因的飲品。

▶ I gained a lot of weight recently. 我最近胖了不少。

oil free 無油；
sugar free
無糖

▶ I'm on a diet. 我在節食中。

▶ I'm a vegetarian. 我吃素。

I feel like having Japanese food today.

Track 018

我今天想吃日本料理。

▶ Does anyone want to eat Korean food?
有人想吃韓國料理嗎？

▶ Who would like to have Indian food?
誰想吃印度菜？

Come on, the restaurant has a bad ◀ *Track 019* reputation.
拜託，那家餐廳評價很差。

▶ You don't really want to go there, do you?
你不是真的想去那裡吃，對吧？

▶ You can't miss the milkshake here.
你一定要試試這裡的奶昔。

I'd like to make a reservation. ◀ *Track 020*
我想要訂位。

▶ I'd like to cancel my reservation.
我想要取消我的訂位。

▶ Table for three, please.
請給我三人的位子。

▶ I need a child seat, please. 我需要一張兒童椅。

I want a large French fries and a ◀ *Track 021* small coke, please.
我要點一份大份薯條和一杯小杯可樂。

▶ Apple pies will be ready in a minute.
蘋果派馬上就好。

▶ Can I refill the coke?
我的可樂可以續杯嗎？

▶ What flavor of milkshake?
什麼口味的奶昔？

large / medium / small 分別表示餐點的大份、中份及小份。

in a minute 可代換為 right away，immediately 或 soon，皆表「立即」「馬上」的意思。

「可續杯」亦可用形容詞 refillable，如：Is the tea refillable? 茶能續杯嗎？

Sorry, the cheeseburger is sold out. ◀ *Track 022*
抱歉，起司漢堡賣完了。

▶ Sorry, we don't have any more cheeseburgers.
抱歉，起司漢堡賣完了。

▶ The fish burger is also a good choice.
魚堡也是個不錯的選擇。

- -

Sorry, I just spilt my coke. ◀ *Track 023*
抱歉，我剛才把可樂灑出來了。

▶ Excuse me, would you please clean the table?
不好意思，可以幫我清潔一下桌面嗎？

用餐禮儀

你可以這樣問

Do you see the no smoking sign over there? ◀ *Track 024*
你看到那裡的禁菸標誌了嗎？

▶ We are in a non-smoking area.
我們在非吸菸區。

cut in line
插隊

▶ Let's wait in line. 我們來排隊吧。

▶ I'm afraid you can't take photos here. 這裡不能拍照。

- -

Cash or charge? ◀ *Track 025*

▶ I'll pay in cash. 我付現金。

▶ Sorry, the credit card is not available.
抱歉，這張信用卡無法使用。

▶ Where's the nearest ATM?
最近的提款機在哪？

「現金不足」可
用 short on cash
表示。

 Would you pass me the pepper? ◀ *Track 026*

請將胡椒遞給我。

▶ Please pass the salt to Jenny.
請將鹽遞給珍妮。

▶ I can't reach the potatoes.
我拿不到馬鈴薯。

 What should I prepare for the ◀ *Track 027*

potluck party?

一人一菜的聚會我該準備什麼？

▶ Let's have a barbeque party.
我們來辦個烤肉派對吧！

▶ It seems that we prepared too much.
我們好像準備太多了。

▶ I am very picky about food.　我很挑食。

你可以這樣說

 Wash your hands before you eat. ◀ *Track 028*

用餐前先洗手。

▶ Stop playing with your knife and fork.
不要再玩你的刀叉了。

▶ Place the napkin on your lap.
將餐巾放在大腿上。

▶ You should eat with chopsticks.
你應該用筷子吃。

「當眾」亦可使用 in public，表示「在公共場合」。in private 則是「私下」的意思。

Don't talk with your mouth full.
Track 029

嘴裡有食物不要說話。

▶ Don't stuff your mouth full of food.
不要把嘴巴塞滿食物。

▶ It's very rude to do that.
那樣是很沒禮貌的。

▶ It's not appropriate to speak so loudly here.
這裡不適合大聲說話。

make a toast 敬酒，正式的西方聚會常有此禮儀，即賓客或主人舉起酒杯和大家說話。

Bottoms up!
Track 030

乾杯！

▶ Cheers! 乾杯！

Check, please.
Track 031

請給我帳單。

bill 亦可作為帳單的意思

▶ Where's the cashier? 請問結帳櫃檯在哪裡？

▶ Where should I pay the bill? 我該去哪裡付帳？

We want separate checks.
Track 032

我們要分開付。

▶ Let's go Dutch. 我們各付各的吧。

It's my treat.
Track 033

我請客。

▶ I'll take care of it. 我來買單。

▶ The dinner is on me. 這頓晚餐算我的。

Eat up! ◀ *Track 034*

吃吧!

▶ Enjoy it! 享受它吧!

▶ Take your time. 慢慢來。

NOTE

· ·

· ·

· ·

· ·

· ·

· ·

· ·

· ·

Chapter 02　生活

「白天」

你可以這樣問

💬 Why didn't you wake me up?　◀ *Track 035*

你為什麼沒有叫我起來？

sharp 的本意
是「尖銳的、
鋒利的」，
這裡是指「整
點」的意思。

▶ I'm late because you didn't wake me up on time.
我要遲到了，都是因為你沒有準時叫我起床。

▶ You were supposed to wake me up at seven o'clock sharp.
你應該要七點整叫我起床的。

・・

💬 What should I wear today?　◀ *Track 036*

今天要穿什麼呢？

▶ I don't know what to wear.
我不知道要穿什麼。

spend ＋時間
＋ on ＋事情
＝ 花多少時間
做某事。

▶ I always spend a long time on deciding what to wear.
我總是花很長的時間來決定要穿什麼衣服。

・・

你可以這樣說

💬 My alarm clock didn't go off this morning.　◀ *Track 037*

今天早上我的鬧鐘沒有響。

▶ I don't think I heard my alarm clock go off.
我覺得我沒有聽到鬧鐘響。

▶ I forgot to set my alarm clock last night.
我昨晚忘記設鬧鐘了。

・・

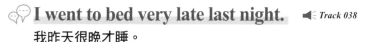

I went to bed very late last night. ◀ *Track 038*

我昨天很晚才睡。

▶ I stayed up late until 2 a.m.
　我凌晨兩點才睡。

▶ I didn't fall asleep until dawn.
　我直到天亮才睡著。

> 「didn't ＋原形動詞＋ until ＋時間」的意思是「直到某時才做某事」。

I need a cup of coffee to wake up. ◀ *Track 039*

我需要喝杯咖啡才能清醒。

▶ Please give me a cup of morning coffee.
　請給我一杯早晨咖啡。

▶ I'm not awake until I've had my coffee.
　我一定要喝了咖啡才會清醒。

> 早上的這杯咖啡稱之為 morning coffee。

Let me sleep for five more minutes. ◀ *Track 040*

讓我再睡五分鐘。

▶ Give me another five minutes.
　再給我五分鐘。

> Let 在本句中是「使役動詞」。

I can't find my blue tie. ◀ *Track 041*

我找不到我的藍色領帶。

▶ Do you know where my white shirt is?
　你知道我的白襯衫在哪裡嗎？

▶ My black pants are not in the closet.
　我的黑色長褲不在衣櫥裡。

It's very cold today. Put on more clothes.

🔊 *Track 042*

今天很冷，要多穿一點。

had better 的意思是「最好是……」，用於已知某種特定狀況，而給他人建議時所使用。

▶ You had better put on your turtleneck.
你最好把高領毛衣穿上。

▶ Don't forget your gloves.
別忘了手套。

There's a missing button at the front.

🔊 *Track 043*

前面有一顆釦子掉了。

inside out 的意思是「裡面跑到外面」，表示裡外相反的意思。

▶ Your fly is open.
你褲子的拉鍊沒拉。

▶ Your t-shirt is inside out.
你的 T 恤穿反了。

I overslept and missed my stop.

🔊 *Track 044*

我睡過站了。

▶ How come the bus is so roomy today?
今天的公車怎麼那麼空啊？

▶ I jumped onto the wrong bus this morning.
我今天早上搭錯公車了。

Gotta run.

🔊 *Track 045*

我得走了。

gotta = got to，是口語的用法。

▶ I've got a train to catch. 我還要趕火車呢。

▶ I have to catch the next bus.
我得搭下一班公車。

We're stuck in the traffic. 🔊 *Track 046*

我們塞在車陣中了。

▶ There won't be so much traffic if we leave ten minutes earlier.
如果我們早十分鐘出門的話，就不會那麼塞了。

▶ I hate to be stuck in the traffic jam every day.
我討厭每天要被塞在車陣中。

晚間

你可以這樣問

Got any plans tonight? 🔊 *Track 047*

今晚有什麼計劃嗎？

▶ Do you have a date tonight?
你今晚有約會嗎？

▶ Have you got anything to do after work?
你下班後有沒有要做什麼？

Do you want a ride? 🔊 *Track 048*

你要搭便車嗎？

▶ Walk me to the bus stop.
陪我走到公車站牌。

▶ My husband is picking me up downstairs.
我先生在樓下要接我。

你可以這樣說

💬 **Let's call it a day.** 🔊 *Track 049*

今天就到此為止了。

▶ I need to leave on time today.
　我今天要準時離開。

on time 準時；
in time 及時

▶ It's been such a long day. 今天真是漫長的一天。

💬 **I have a date with my boyfriend** 🔊 *Track 050*
tonight.

我今天晚上要跟我男朋友約會。

一般簡單的
晚餐稱為
supper，這邊
用 dinner 表示
可能是家庭性
的聚餐，為較
正式的晚餐。

▶ I'm having dinner with my family.
　我要跟家人一起吃晚餐。

💬 **I have English conversation classes** 🔊 *Track 051*
on Tuesday nights.

星期二晚上我有英文會話課。

▶ I don't have any particular plans for tonight.
　我今晚沒有什麼特別的計畫。

💬 **I need to work overtime today.** 🔊 *Track 052*

我今天要加班。

▶ I have to finish this report before I go.
　我離開前要把這份報告完成。

▶ I've been working late this week.
　我這一整個星期都在加班。

▶ We don't get paid for working overtime.
　我們加班沒有加班費。

Let's dine out tonight.

🔊 *Track 053*

我們今晚到外面吃吧。

▶ I'm too tired to cook.
我太累了不想煮飯。

▶ Let's order takeout.
我們來叫外賣吧。

> too...to... 的用法表示「太⋯⋯以致於不⋯⋯」。

My favorite TV program is starting in five minutes.

🔊 *Track 054*

我最喜歡的電視節目還有五分鐘就要開始了。

▶ Who remembers what happened in the last episode?
誰記得上一集發生了什麼事？

▶ I've seen this episode. This is a rerun.
我看過這一集了。這是重播。

I want to take a nice bath.

🔊 *Track 055*

我要泡個舒服的澡。

▶ I think a hot bath will help me relax.
我想泡個熱水澡應該可以幫助我放鬆一下。

▶ I'm so tired that I want to skip shower and go to bed.
我太累了不想淋浴了，直接睡覺去。

> bath 是指在浴缸裡「泡澡」，「淋浴」則是 take a shower。

My eyelids are heavy already.

🔊 *Track 056*

我的眼皮已經很沉重了。

▶ I might fall asleep any minute.
我隨時都有可能睡著。

▶ I keep yawning. 我一直打哈欠。

I don't need to go to work tomorrow, great!

◀ *Track 057*

明天不用上班，太好了！

▶ It's great that I don't need to get up early tomorrow.
明天不用早起真是太好了。

▶ I have an early day tomorrow.
我明天要早起。

Don't forget to set the alarm clock. ◀ *Track 058*

別忘了設定鬧鐘。

▶ Please keep the night light on.
請把小夜燈開著。

▶ Did you check the door?
你有檢查門鎖了沒了嗎？

「大眾運輸」

你可以這樣問

💬 **Where does this bus go?** 🔊 *Track 059*

這輛公車是到哪？

▶ Which bus should we take?
我們應該搭幾號公車？

▶ I think I'm going in the wrong direction.
我覺得我好像坐錯方向了。

▶ Is this my stop? 這是我要下車的站嗎？

💬 **Does this bus go to the City Library?** 🔊 *Track 060*

這輛公車有到市立圖書館嗎？

▶ Which stop should I get off at?
我應該在哪一站下車？

▶ How much is the fare? 車資多少？

▶ Do I pay now or when I get off?
我是現在付錢，還是下車時付？

▶ Where should I transfer?
我應該在哪裡換車？

你可以這樣說

💬 **Let's take a taxi.** 🔊 *Track 061*

我們搭計程車吧。

▶ How long does it take to go to the City Hall?
到市政府需要多久時間？

▶ Please drop me off at the second traffic light.
請在第二個紅綠燈的地方放我下來。

💬 **Public transit in Taipei is very convenient.** ◀ *Track 062*

台北市的大眾運輸系統非常方便。

▶ It saves a lot of time to go from place to place.
為兩地之間的交通節省不少時間。

▶ I can hardly recall the days without the MRT.
我已經很難想起過去沒有捷運的日子。

· ·

💬 **It is very convenient to take the MRT in Taipei.** ◀ *Track 063*

在台北搭乘捷運非常方便。

▶ You can get an IC token from the vending machine.
可以從販賣機購買 IC 代幣。

▶ With a one-day pass you can take unlimited rides within the service day.
一日票在當營業日可無限次乘坐。

▶ There's also a single journey ticket for cyclists.
騎腳踏車的人也可以購買自行車單程票。

▶ For frequent riders you can also get an EasyCard.
經常搭乘捷運的人可購買悠遊卡。

· ·

💬 **I have to rush for the first train every day.** ◀ *Track 064*

我每天都要趕著搭第一班火車。

▶ I have to squash myself into the train.
我得把自己擠進車廂。

▶ The trains are always jammed in the morning.
早上火車總是塞得滿滿的。

· ·

The HSR has become another popular form of transportation in Taiwan.

🔊 *Track 065*

台灣的高鐵已成為另一種大眾運輸方式。

▶ Many business people travel back and forth by HSR every day.
很多商務人士每天利用高鐵南來北往。

▶ HSR shortens the distance between Taipei and Kaohsiung.
高鐵縮短了台北與高雄間的距離。

> HSR 是台灣高鐵的簡稱，全名為 Taiwan High Speed Rail，因此也稱作 THSR。

I want to book an HSR ticket online.

🔊 *Track 066*

我要上網訂一張高鐵票。

▶ You'll need the number to pick up the tickets.
你需要訂位代號來取票。

▶ Did you print out the reservation confirmation page?
你有沒有把確認訂位的頁面列印下來？

▶ Have you completed the payment procedures?
你完成付款流程了嗎？

▶ You can book a ticket 15 days prior to the travel date.
你可以預訂乘車日前 15 日的車票。

道路駕駛

你可以這樣問

How do I get to your place?

🔊 *Track 067*

我要怎麼到你家去？

▶ Do you know any short cuts to the highway?
你知道通往高速公路的捷徑嗎？

▶ Do you have any idea where the entrance is?
你知不知道入口在哪裡呢？

Are there any landmarks around? ◀ *Track 068*
那附近有沒有明顯的地標？

▶ There's a large roundabout nearby.
旁邊有個很大的圓環。

▶ It's about a one-minute walk from the night market.
從夜市走過去大約一分鐘的時間。

Could you check the brakes for me? ◀ *Track 069*
請你幫我檢查一下煞車好嗎？

▶ I think the hand brake needs to be adjusted.
我覺得手煞車需要調整了。

▶ It's about time to change the brake fluid.
差不多該換煞車油了。

▶ The brake light is not working. 煞車燈故障了。

你可以這樣說

juice 在俚語中有「電」的意思。也可以說 I have a dead battery。

I can't start the engine. ◀ *Track 070*
我沒辦法發動引擎。

▶ There's no juice in the battery. 電瓶沒電了。

▶ What can I do to restart the engine?
我要怎麼樣重新啟動引擎？

▶ I need to call for roadside service.
我得叫道路救援。

jump start 是在國外拿一條接電線（jumper）從別台車接電過來，這個動作就是 jump start。

▶ I have a dead battery. Can you jump start my car?
我的電瓶沒電了。你可以幫我接電嗎？

💬 **I'm almost out of gas.** 🔊 *Track 071*

車子快要沒油了。

▶ Do you know where the nearest gas station is?
你知道最近的加油站在哪裡嗎？

▶ Gas up your car before we get on the highway.
上高速公路以前把油箱加滿。

> gas up 也可用 fuel up 代替，gas 及 fuel 當名詞時都是表示「燃料」的意思，在這裡都是當動詞用。

💬 **I got a ticket for speeding.** 🔊 *Track 072*

我收到一張超速罰單。

▶ I didn't see the traffic signal change.
我沒有看到紅綠燈變換。

▶ Please drive within the speed limit.
請在速限內駕駛。

▶ I was fined three thousand dollars.
我被開了張三千元的罰單。

> speed 一般當成名詞使用，表示「速度」。speeding 中的 speed 是動詞，表示「超速駕駛」時通常以動名詞表示。

> fine 在這裡當動詞，表示「處以……罰金」。

💬 **My car was towed.** 🔊 *Track 073*

我的車被拖吊了。

▶ I have a flat tire. 我的車子爆胎了。

💬 **Let's go for a ride!** 🔊 *Track 074*

我們開車去兜風吧。

▶ Fasten your seatbelt! 繫上安全帶。

💬 **Walk down this road.** 🔊 *Track 075*

沿著這條街走。

▶ Go straight ahead for three blocks.
直走三條街。

▶ Turn left at the post office.
在郵局那邊左轉。

▶ You'll see the bank on the right.
你就會看到銀行在右手邊。

The bookstore is across from the supermarket.
◀ *Track 076*

書店在超市的對面。

▶ It's next to the pharmacy.
在藥局的旁邊。

▶ It's between the restaurant and the fruit stand.
它在餐廳和水果店的中間。

▶ Go past the police station and you'll see it.
走過警察局你就會看到了。

I'm sorry. I don't know the way.
◀ *Track 077*

對不起。我不知道路。

▶ I'm a stranger here myself.
我對這邊也不熟。

▶ I'm new here as well. 我也剛到這裡。

Watch out for speed traps around here.
◀ *Track 078*

注意這附近的測速照相喔。

▶ Slow down! There's a speed camera ahead!
慢一點！前面有測速照相機。

▶ I don't want to pay for another speeding ticket.
我可不想再付超速罰單了。

trap 是「陷阱」，抓測速的陷阱，也就是「測速照相」。

You forgot to give a turn signal. ◀ *Track 079*

你忘了打方向燈了。

▶ It is very important to follow the traffic rules.
遵守交通規則是非常重要的。

▶ Hey, did you just ignore that red light?
嘿，你剛才闖紅燈是嗎？

- -

The sign says you can't make a U turn here. ◀ *Track 080*

告示牌說你不能在這邊迴轉。

▶ This road is closed to all vehicles.
這條路禁止所有車輛通行。

▶ Take the inner lane.
走內線車道。

▶ You have to give way here.
你在這裡要讓一下。

> inner lane 是內線車道，outer lane 是外線車道。

> 車子迴轉就像是字母 U 的寫法一樣，來個 180 度大轉彎，因此「迴轉」就叫 U turn。

- -

Pedestrians should take the crosswalk when crossing streets. ◀ *Track 081*

行人過馬路應該走行人穿越道。

▶ Jaywalking is dangerous.
穿越馬路是危險的。

▶ You should look in both directions before crossing the street.
過馬路前應該要看一下兩側。

> 「斑馬線」的英文是 zebra crossing，而 crosswalk 可泛指所有的「行人穿越道」。

> jaywalk 是指「不遵守交通規則，任意穿越馬路」。

「室內居家」

你可以這樣問

Do you think I need to replace my sofa?

🔊 *Track 082*

你覺得我要換沙發嗎？

loveseat 表示「二人座的沙發」的意思。

▶ Do you like my new loveseat?
你喜歡我新買的雙人沙發嗎？

couch 表示「三人座（以上）的沙發」的意思。

▶ What do you think of my new couch?
你認為我的沙發如何？

Where is the dishwashing liquid?

🔊 *Track 083*

洗碗精放在哪裡？

dishwashing liquid 表示「洗碗精」的意思。

▶ The blender is in the cabinet. 果汁機放在儲物櫃裡。

Did I leave my watch in there?

🔊 *Track 084*

我有把手錶放在裡面嗎？

▶ Did I hang the towel on the towel rack?
我有把毛巾掛在毛巾架上嗎？

Would you please hurry up and come out?

🔊 *Track 085*

可以快一點出來嗎？

▶ You took too long in the bathroom.
你在廁所花太多時間了。

▶ You take forever in the washroom.
你佔用廁所的時間太久了。

How long is the warranty period? ◀ *Track 086*

保固期有多久？

▶ It offers two years of warranty.
　這提供兩年保固。

▶ The warranty period for this TV is two years.
　這台電視機的保固有兩年。

．．．．．．．．．．．．．．．．．．．．．．．．．．．．．．．．．．

你可以這樣說

I am going to rearrange the living room. ◀ *Track 087*

我要重新佈置客廳的擺設。

▶ The living room needs to be renovated.
　客廳要重新裝潢了。

▶ I want to put the TV unit against the wall.
　我要把電視櫃放到牆邊。

．．．．．．．．．．．．．．．．．．．．．．．．．．．．．．．．．．

I want to hang the pictures on the wall. ◀ *Track 088*

我想把這些照片掛在牆上。

▶ The painting on the wall is very special.
　掛在牆上的照片很別緻。

▶ The color of your curtain matches your wall.
　你家窗簾跟牆的顏色很搭。

．．．．．．．．．．．．．．．．．．．．．．．．．．．．．．．．．．

Please put the cans in the recycle bin.

Track 089

請把罐子丟到回收筒裡。

garbage disposal 為一種將廚餘碾碎並排到下水道的裝置。

▶ We don't have the garbage disposal.
我們沒有垃圾處理機。

▶ Don't put the leftovers on the counter.
不要把廚餘丟在流理台上。

Please hang this coat in the closet.

Track 090

請把外套掛到衣櫥裡。

closet 表示「大型的衣櫥」，dresser 指的是「有抽屜的衣櫃」。walk-in closet 則是指「更衣間」。

▶ Please dust the dresser.
請把衣櫃的灰塵清一清。

The bathroom is occupied.

Track 091

廁所裡有人。

nature calls 在此表示「想上廁所」的意思。

▶ Nature calls. 我要去上洗手間。

▶ I need to use the toilet. 我要去上洗手間。

I can't live without an air conditioner in summer.

Track 092

我夏天不能沒有冷氣。

▶ Can you check if the fan is working?
你可以檢查一下電扇有在動嗎？

▶ I think there are some problems with the remote control.
我覺得遙控器有問題。

▶ The laundry machine needs repair.
這洗衣機該修理了。

Check the instructions in the manual.

Track 093

看一下說明書上的使用方法。

▶ This brand is trustworthy.
這個牌子很可靠。

▶ I want to pay by installments.
我要分期付款。

The power is running low.

Track 094

快沒電了。

▶ The power is out. 停電了。

▶ The battery is dead. 電池沒電了。

▶ The power is back on. 復電了。

The sink is leaking.

Track 095

水槽在漏水。

▶ My light is blinking strangely.
我的電燈異常地閃爍。

▶ The paint of the wall is peeling.
牆上的漆漸漸掉落。

I haven't got a solution for the cockroaches.

Track 096

我還沒找到消滅蟑螂的辦法。

▶ High humidity in homes causes a variety of health
problems.
過於潮濕的房子會引發各種疾病

cause 引發、
造成

▶ Mold is a big problem of this house.
黴菌是這間房子最大的問題。

▶ I feel there are fleas everywhere in the house.
　我感覺這房子到處都是跳蚤。

· ·

My toilet is stuck.　　　　　　　　◀ Track 097
我的馬桶塞住了。

yellow pages
電話簿

▶ Check the yellow pages to get some help.
　查一查電話簿去找人幫忙。

· ·

I want to get rid of the old furniture. ◀ Track 098
我想把老舊的傢俱丟掉。
▶ The stains on the curtain are very hard to remove.
　這窗簾上的污漬很難去掉。

「室外環境」

你可以這樣問

Where's the nearest drug store?　　◀ Track 099
最近的藥房在哪裡？
▶ Is there any supermarket around?
　這附近有超級市場嗎？
▶ Is there a post office near here?　這附近有郵局嗎？
▶ Is there a bank nearby?　這附近有銀行嗎？

· ·

你可以這樣說

Here comes the garbage truck.　　◀ Track 100
垃圾車來了。

▶ The garbage truck comes around 8 o'clock.
垃圾車大約八點來。

▶ The dustmen are collecting the rubbish.
清潔人員正在收垃圾。

The new mall has an opening sale. ◀ *Track 101*

新的購物中心有開幕優惠。

▶ There's a new Japanese restaurant next to the bakery.
在麵包店隔壁新開了一間日本料理店。

The dog next door has been barking all day long. ◀ *Track 102*

隔壁的狗整天都在叫。

▶ The cars bother me a lot.
那些車對我造成嚴重的困擾。

▶ They make lots of noise every night.
他們每晚都製造很多噪音。

My new apartment is not far from the train station. ◀ *Track 103*

我的新公寓離火車站不遠。

▶ I need a place with a great location.
我需要一個在好地段的住處。

▶ I like the place for the neighborhood is quiet and clean.
我喜歡這附近安靜又整潔的環境。

Late night parties are not allowed. ◀ *Track 104*

不允許晚上開派對。

▶ It's not permitted to raise pets here.
這裡不能養寵物。

▶ It's not convenient to keep a dog here.
這裡不方便養狗。

I'm looking for a female roommate. ◀ *Track 105*

我在找一名女室友。

landlady
女房東；
tenant 房客

▶ My landlord is a nice person.
我的房東是個好人。

▶ Is the house for rent or for sale?
這房子是要租還是要賣？

flat 和
apartment 皆
為「公寓」的
意思，flat 是
英式用法。

▶ Bob and I share a flat.
鮑伯和我一起租公寓。

身體不適

你可以這樣問

💬 Are you OK?

🔈 *Track 106*

你還好嗎？

▶ Is everything alright?
　一切都還好嗎？

▶ What's wrong with you?
　你怎麼了？

▶ Do you need some rest?
　你需要休息一下嗎？

💬 Do you have a pain-killer?

🔈 *Track 107*

你有止痛藥嗎？

▶ I need to take some aspirin.
　我要吃一些阿斯匹靈。

▶ Where can I get some medicine?
　我可以去哪裡買藥？

> killer 原意是「殺手」，pain-killer 疼痛殺手，也可以解釋成「頭痛藥」。

> medicine 泛指所有的藥品，pill 是「藥丸」。

💬 How can I get rid of my stress?

🔈 *Track 108*

我該如何擺脫壓力？

▶ Taking a vacation will help relief your stress.
　度假能幫助你減輕壓力。

▶ Talking to your friends can also ease your tension.
　和朋友聊聊也能舒緩你的壓力。

▶ Taking exercise is also good for reducing stress.
　運動也對降低壓力很有幫助。

> get rid of ＋名詞 / 動詞 ing... 擺脫......

> relief / ease 都有「緩和、減緩」之意；reduce 則有「減輕、降低」之意。

> tension 指精神上的「緊繃」，亦有「壓力」之意。

Can I talk to my doctor?
Track 109
我可以和醫生談一談嗎？

▶ Don't forget to take your medicine on time.
別忘了要準時吃藥。

Could you please tell me where the emergency room is?
Track 110
請問急診室在哪？

▶ Where is the operation room?
手術室在哪裡？

▶ Please go to the medicine counter to get your medicine.
請到領藥處領藥。

你可以這樣說

You don't look well to me.
Track 111
你看起來不太好。

▶ I don't feel well. 我覺得不太舒服。

▶ Are you feeling better now?
你現在覺得好點了嗎？

表達身體「好不好？」不可以用 good，而是要用 well 這個字。

I feel weak and sluggish.
Track 112
我覺得很虛弱和倦怠。

▶ I felt dizzy and fatigue from this morning.
從早上開始我就覺得頭暈又疲倦。

▶ I broke out in a skin rash and got a fever.
我身上起了疹子而且發燒。

sluggish 倦怠的、有氣無力的；dizzy 暈眩的；fatigue 疲倦的

skin rash 皮膚起疹；broke out 起、長

I have a sore throat.

Track 113

我喉嚨痛。

▶ I have a fever and a running nose. 我發燒又流鼻水。

▶ My headache is killing me. 我的頭痛死了。

ache 表示「疼痛」的意思，通常和疼痛部位合成一個單字來表示。例如：toothache 牙痛。

I'll help you register at a hospital.

Track 114

我先幫你掛號。

▶ How much is the registration fee?

掛號費多少錢？

Get well soon.

Track 115

祝你早日康復。

▶ Take care. 保重。

▶ May God bless you. 願主保佑你。

如果聽到有人打噴嚏時，也可以對他說 Bless you.

I have been sleepless for three nights.

Track 116

我已經失眠三天了。

▶ I envy those who fall asleep easily.

我好羨慕那些能倒頭就睡的人。

My grandpa has suffered from diabetes for more than ten years.

Track 117

我爺爺已經罹患糖尿病超過十年了。

▶ He has to get a shot of insulin three times a day.

他必須每天注射胰島素三次。

▶ He has to measure his blood sugar after meals.

他必須在飯後測量血糖。

suffer from ＋疾病為「罹患……」之意

diabetes 糖尿病；diabetic 糖尿病的；blood sugar 血糖；measure the blood sugar 量血糖

treatment
治療

She's trying a series of treatments for her depression.　◀ *Track 118*

她正在嘗試一連串的憂鬱症療程。

psychiatrist
精神科醫師；
shrink 則為
俗稱。

▶ She goes to see a psychiatrist twice a week.
她一週去看精神科醫師兩次。

consult
諮詢、會診；
counseling 心
理諮商

▶ After consulting a shrink with her problems, she felt better.
向心理醫生諮詢過後，她覺得好多了。

• •

I'm going to be discharged from hospital tomorrow.　◀ *Track 119*

我明天就可以出院了。

醫美健檢

你可以這樣問

Where should I go for a health examination?　◀ *Track 120*

我該到哪裡做健康檢查？

▶ We should get health examinations regularly.
我們應該定期做健康檢查。

• •

你可以這樣說

My blood type is O.　◀ *Track 121*

我的血型是 O 型。

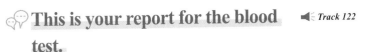
▶ Which is your blood type?
你的血型是哪一種？

▶ You need to fill in your blood type in the form.
你需要在表格內填入血型。

> fill in 表示「填入」的意思。

🗨 This is your report for the blood test. ◀ Track 122

這是你的驗血報告。

▶ Is everything OK on my report for the blood test?
我的驗血結果正常嗎？

▶ We need to wait for your report for the blood test.
我們必須等你的驗血報告出來。

🗨 I made a reservation for a two-day health examination package. ◀ Track 123

我預約了兩天的健康檢查。

▶ I don't have time to get a two-day examination.
我沒有時間做兩天的健康檢查。

▶ What are the basic items in the health examination?
健康檢查的基本項目有哪些？

🗨 I'm going to the hospital with my wife for her prenatal examination next Tuesday. ◀ Track 124

下週二我要陪我太太去醫院產檢。

▶ When is the estimated date of delivery?
預產期是什麼時候？

> be going to 表示「將要……」的意思。

The liver function is one of the most important items.

Track 125

肝功能是重要的項目之一。

▶ You have to do some further examinations.
　你必須要做更進一步的檢查。

one of 表示
「其中之一」
的意思。

My doctor suggested me to have a gastroscopy.

Track 126

醫生建議我做胃鏡檢查。

▶ Will I feel uncomfortable during the gastroscopy?
　照胃鏡的時候會不舒服嗎？

uncomfortable
表示「不舒
服」的意思；
相反詞是
comfortable
「舒服」。

Fraxel Laser is one of the new techniques for beauty treatment.

Track 127

飛梭是一項新的美容技術。

▶ How long will it take for my inflamed skin to recover?
　我的皮膚紅腫多久會恢復？

How long...?
表示「多久？」
的意思。

I want to do a double-fold eyelid operation.

Track 128

我想要割雙眼皮。

▶ I don't like my flat nose.
　我不喜歡我的塌鼻子。

Micro-plastic surgeries are very popular these years.
Track 129

這些年微整形非常受歡迎。

▶ My parents can't accept if I go to improve my looks.
我爸媽不接受我去整形。

• •

It is easy to have acne on the face in puberty.
Track 130

青春期臉上容易長粉刺。

▶ The pimple is getting bigger and bigger.
這顆青春痘愈來愈大。

▶ The pimple has disappeared.
那顆青春痘消了。

> bigger and bigger
> 表示「愈來愈大」
> 的意思。

Chapter 06　婚喪喜慶

「節慶」

你可以這樣問

Where are we going to celebrate Christmas?

◀ *Track 131*

聖誕節要去哪狂歡？

▶ I've already planned to do something special for Christmas Eve.
我已經計畫好聖誕夜要做點特別的事。

▶ What's your plan for Christmas?
聖誕節你有什麼計畫？

・・・・・・・・・・・・・・・・・・・・・・・・・・・・・・・・・・・・・

Are you going home for Chinese New Year?

◀ *Track 132*

農曆新年你要回鄉嗎？

▶ It's hard to get a train ticket.
火車票好難買。

get together
表示「聚在一
起」的意思。

▶ Will you get together with you family during New Year holidays?
過年會和家人一起嗎？

・・・・・・・・・・・・・・・・・・・・・・・・・・・・・・・・・・・・・

Are you going to watch the fireworks?

◀ *Track 133*

你要一起去看煙火嗎？

about to 表示
「正要……」，
不是「大約」
的意思。

▶ I'm about to go for the fireworks.
我正要去看煙火。

▶ Where are you going for the New Year's party?
你要去哪裡參加跨年晚會？

・・・・・・・・・・・・・・・・・・・・・・・・・・・・・・・・・・・・・

💬 Do you have a day off on Labor Day?

◀ *Track 134*

勞動節你有放假嗎？

▶ I have to go to work on Labor Day.
我勞動節要上班。

▶ Do you work on Labor Day?
你勞動節要上班嗎？

> have to 是「必須」的意思。

你可以這樣說

💬 I'm going to enjoy the sight of the parade.

◀ *Track 135*

我要去看遊行。

▶ Are you invited to go to the celebration?
你有被邀請去參加慶典嗎？

💬 I ate too many moon cakes.

◀ *Track 136*

我吃太多月餅了。

💬 I usually go tomb sweeping with my family on Tomb Sweeping Day.

◀ *Track 137*

清明節我通常會和家人去掃墓。

▶ Will you go tomb sweeping this year?
你今年要去掃墓嗎？。

▶ Do you usually go home on Tomb Sweeping Day?
你通常清明節會回鄉嗎？

🗨 I bought some chocolate for Valentine's Day.

🔊 *Track 138*

我買了一些情人節巧克力。

▶ Did you receive any chocolate on Valentine's Day?
你情人節有收到巧克力嗎？

🗨 I enjoy costume parties.

🔊 *Track 139*

我喜歡化妝舞會。

▶ Did you rent a costume for Halloween?
你有去租萬聖節服裝嗎？

▶ Trick or treat! 不給糖就搗蛋！

Trick or treat. 是萬聖節活動，小朋友討糖果時說的話。

🗨 My mom made some rice cakes on the Dragon Boat Festival this year.

🔊 *Track 140*

我媽媽今年端午節包了一些粽子。

rice cake 表示「粽子」，也可以直接說 Tzung-Tzu。

喪禮

你可以這樣問

🗨 Did he have a will?

🔊 *Track 141*

他有留下遺書嗎？

▶ We're going to read his will after his funeral.
我們會在他的喪禮之後宣讀他的遺書。

▶ He didn't leave a will.
他沒有留下遺書。

will 表示「遺書」或「遺願」的意思。

你可以這樣說

He was a good man.

Track 142

他生前是個好人。

▶ He was too young to die.
他英年早逝。

. . . .

I couldn't believe that he is gone.

Track 143

我不敢相信他走了。

▶ It can't be possible that he's no longer with us.
他死了，這不是真的吧！

▶ It's hard to accept that he passed away.
他走了，真是讓人難以接受。

> pass away 為「死亡」的意思。

. . . .

I am sorry to hear about his death.

Track 144

他的死，令人感到遺憾。

▶ I am sorry for your loss.
你的損失真令人遺憾。

. . . .

She died peacefully.

Track 145

她很平靜地走了。

▶ She died without pain.
她沒有痛苦的走了。

. . . .

Be strong!

Track 146

堅強點。

▶ Don't cry! 別哭了！

. . . .

I will be there for you.

Track 147

我會在你的身邊支持你。

▶ I am here for support. 我來這裡支持你。

▶ I am here if you need any help.
我來這裡幫忙。

May good memories be in your thoughts.

Track 148

願美好的回憶留在心中。

▶ May you always remember the good times you had.
願你有留下美好的回憶。

▶ She'll always be on your mind.
她會永遠與你們同在。

▶ She'll be remembered as her legacy.
她會像是沒離開過一樣。

May she rest in peace.

Track 149

願她安息。

▶ Rest in peace. 安息。

紀念日

你可以這樣問

How are you going to celebrate?

Track 150

你想怎麼慶祝？

▶ How do you plan to celebrate?
你想如何慶祝？

▶ What do you have in mind for the celebration?
你打算怎麼慶祝？

> have in mind 表示「打算」的意思。

Have you ordered a birthday cake? ◀ *Track 151*

你訂生日蛋糕了嗎？

▶ Did you order a cake? 你有預訂蛋糕嗎？

> order 在此表示「預訂」的意思。

Do you want to come to my birthday party? ◀ *Track 152*

你要來我的生日派對嗎？

▶ I want to invite you to my birthday party.
我想邀請你來我的生日派對。

▶ You're coming to my birthday party, aren't you?
你會來我的生日派對，對吧？

Who is your best man? ◀ *Track 153*

你的伴郎是誰？

▶ Who is the bridesmaid? 你的伴娘是誰？

▶ Can you be my maid of honor? 你可以當我的主伴娘嗎？

▶ My nephew is my pageboy. 我的姪子是我的花童。

Where are you going for your honeymoon? ◀ *Track 154*

你們要去哪裡度蜜月？

▶ We aren't having a honeymoon. 我們沒有要去度蜜月。

▶ We are going to a fancy resort for our honeymoon.
我們要去一個高級的度假村度蜜月。

Where did you take your wedding photos?

Track 155

你們的婚紗照在哪裡拍的？

▶ You look great in your wedding photos.
你的婚紗照照得很美。

What do you want as a gift?

Track 156

你有想要什麼禮物嗎？

▶ Do you want anything as a gift?
你想要什麼東西當作禮物？

▶ Just surprise me! 給我個驚喜吧！

你可以這樣說

My mother's birthday is coming soon.

Track 157

我媽媽的生日快到了。

around the corner 表示「即將來臨」的意思。

▶ My mother's birthday is around the corner.
快到我媽媽的生日了。

I am going to hold a birthday party for her.

Track 158

我要幫她辦個生日派對。

▶ I am thinking of buying her a fancy dress.
我想幫她買件高級的洋裝。

▶ Let's give her a surprise party!
我們來給她一個驚喜派對吧。

He popped the question last night.   ◀ Track 159

他昨晚向我求婚了。

▶ He proposed to me last night.
他昨晚向我求婚。

▶ Will you marry me?
嫁給我好嗎？

> pop 是指東西突然彈跳起來，會讓人嚇一跳的意思。pop the question 則意指為「突然提起某問題」，衍生為「求婚」的意思。

They are made for each other.   ◀ Track 160

他們很相配。

▶ They are the perfect match.
他們很相配。

▶ They're meant to be together.
他們注定要在一起的。

▶ I finally found my other half.
我終於找到我的另一半了。

> Will you marry me? 可同時表示「嫁給我」和「娶我」的意思。

Welcome to our wedding.   ◀ Track 161

歡迎來參加我們的婚禮。

▶ Thanks for coming to our wedding.
謝謝你來參加我們的婚禮。

May you two always be in love.   ◀ Track 162

永浴愛河。

▶ We never knew two people better suited for each other.
你們真是天造地設的一對。

▶ I wish you happiness for the rest of your lives.
百年好合。

💬 Happy anniversary!
🔊 *Track 163*

結婚紀念日快樂。

▶ Today is my grandparents' 50th wedding anniversary.
今天是我祖父母結婚 50 週年紀念日。

* *

💬 He bought me a ring.
🔊 *Track 164*

他買了一枚戒指給我。

▶ He gave me a diamond ring as a gift.
他給了我一枚鑽戒當禮物。

* *

💬 Let's celebrate our first anniversary!
🔊 *Track 165*

我們去慶祝週年紀念日吧！

▶ Let's have a romantic night together.
讓我們有個浪漫的夜晚吧！

NOTE

Part 2

讓你表達自我的
外表內在講法

身體部位

你可以這樣問

💬 **What's that bruise on your face?** 🔊 Track 166

你臉上的瘀青是怎麼回事？

▶ How did you get that bump?
你那邊是怎麼撞到的？

▶ How did you get scratched?
你是怎麼被抓傷的？

- -

你可以這樣說

💬 **Her eyelashes are long.** 🔊 Track 167

她的眼睫毛很長。

▶ I was attracted by her beautiful eyes.
我被她漂亮的眼睛吸引住了。

▶ I never liked my bushy eyebrows.
我從來都沒喜歡過我濃密的眉毛。

當句中有超過兩個形容詞時，其出現的順序為：形狀尺寸→年齡→新舊→顏色。

- -

💬 **I have nose allergies.** 🔊 Track 168

我有鼻子過敏的問題。

▶ I have a runny nose. 我在流鼻水。

▶ I have a stuffy nose. 我鼻塞。

▶ Excuse me. I need to blow my nose.
抱歉，我要擤一下鼻涕。

▶ You should see an ENT doctor.
你應該要去看耳鼻喉科。

stuff 當動詞是「填塞」，字尾＋ y 變成形容詞，表示「塞住的」的

ENT = Ear Nose Throat。耳鼻喉

I have a dandruff problem.
Track 169

我有頭皮屑的困擾。

▶ Don't pick your nose in front of me.
不要在我面前挖鼻孔。

▶ I hate the freckles on my face.
我討厭我臉上的雀斑。

▶ I adore the dimples when she smiles.
我喜歡她微笑時臉上的酒窩。

Take a look at my biceps.
Track 170

看看我的二頭肌。

▶ I saw Jack and Rose walking in the park arm in arm.
我看到傑克與蘿絲兩個人手挽著手在公園散步。

I'm left-handed.
Track 171

我是左撇子。

▶ I shook hands with the President!
我和總統握手耶！

▶ The teacher snapped her fingers to get the students'attention.
老師彈了一下手指來吸引學生們的注意力。

握手的英文是
shake hands。

▶ Let's give them a big hand. 讓我們為他們鼓掌。

Don't cross your legs.
Track 172

不要蹺二郎腿。

▶ Don't sit with your legs crossed. 坐著的時候不要盤腿。

▶ My legs are sore. 我的腿很痠。

I hit my funny bone.

Track 173

我撞到手肘了。

▶ I sprained my wrist.
我的手腕扭到了。

funny bone 是「手肘的尺骨端」，因碰撞到會有麻痛、不舒服的感覺，英文說是一種 funny feeling（哭笑不得的感覺），故名為 funny bone。

I often get cramps on my calves in the morning.

Track 174

我的小腿常在早上抽筋。

▶ I banged my knee against the table.
我的膝蓋撞到桌子了。

period 表示「週期、期間」，在這邊表示「生理期」的意思。

I sprained my ankle.

Track 175

我扭到腳踝了。

▶ I have a serious period pain.
我生理痛很嚴重。

▶ I'm suffering from athlete's foot.
我飽受香港腳之苦。

香港腳就是「足癬」，英文是 athlete's foot。

I have a corn on my right foot.

Track 176

我右腳上有雞眼。

▶ I wear high heels every day. That's why I have corns on my feet.
我每天穿高跟鞋，所以兩隻腳都有雞眼。

▶ Please buy some corn plaster for me.
請幫我買些雞眼的貼布。

外貌體型

你可以這樣問

💬 **What can I do to improve my body shape?**　◀ *Track 177*

我能做什麼來改善身材呢？

▶ Regular exercise will keep you in good shape.
規律的運動可以幫助你保持好身材。

▶ Exercise also lets me burn off stress from work.
運動也幫助我舒解工作壓力。

你可以這樣說

💬 **I lost a few kilos after I changed my diet habits.**　◀ *Track 178*

我改變飲食習慣後，瘦了幾公斤。

▶ Try to have a healthy and balanced diet.
請試著飲食均衡健康。

▶ I'm on a diet. 我正在節食中。

💬 **I gained a few kilos because of my irregular lifestyle.**　◀ *Track 179*

我因為生活作息不正常，胖了幾公斤。

▶ I've been working late and having night snacks.
我最近常加班又吃宵夜。

▶ I want to get rid of the fat around my stomach.
我想要消除腹部的贅肉。

You look cute.

Track 180

你看起來很可愛。

▶ The girl looks hot. 那女孩看起來很性感。

▶ That man is really good-looking. 那個男人很好看。

> hot 與 sexy 都可用來形容人看起來很「性感」，男女皆通用。

Don't slouch.

Track 181

不要彎腰駝背。

▶ Stand up straight. 請抬頭挺胸站好。

> slouch 就是看起來「無精打采」的樣子。

I don't like to wear makeup.

Track 182

我不喜歡化妝。

▶ I only wear a little makeup on work days.
我上班的時候只畫淡妝。

▶ I never go out without putting on makeup.
我沒化妝絕不出門。

▶ Jenny always wears heavy makeup.
珍妮總是化濃妝。

> 「化妝」可用 wear 或 put on 加 makeup。

You have a good complexion.

Track 183

你的氣色很好。

▶ You look pale today. 你今天看起來臉很蒼白。

She reminds me of my grandmother.

Track 184

她讓我想起我祖母。

▶ I don't like his arrogant look.
我不喜歡他那自大的表情。

▶ He looks so much like a movie star.
他看來很像一個電影明星。

I hate my curly hair.

◀ Track 185

我討厭我的捲髮。

▶ My hair is naturally curly.
我的頭髮是自然捲。

▶ I want to get my hair straightened.
我想要把頭髮燙直。

> straight 是形容詞，表示「直的」，字尾＋en 後變成動詞，表示「把……弄直」的意思。

I'm getting bald.

◀ Track 186

我快要禿頭了。

▶ I'm losing my hair. 我一直掉頭髮。

▶ I'm thinking about getting some plugs.
我在考慮要植髮。

▶ Do you think I should wear a wig?
你覺得我該戴假髮嗎？

> bald 可用來形容「禿頭的」或「禿的、光禿禿的」。

> plug 可表示「接上……」。

I want to change my hairstyle.

◀ Track 187

我想要換個新髮型。

▶ I want to perm my hair.
我想把頭髮燙一下。

▶ How do you like my new hairstyle?
你覺得我的新髮型怎麼樣？

> trim 是指「修剪」，在這裡指「依照原來髮型做修剪而已」。

Bangs are in fashion this year.

◀ Track 188

瀏海是今年最流行的髮型。

▶ I want to get my hair trimmed.
我想要修剪一下頭髮。

▶ Your new hairstyle fits your face well.
你的新髮型很適合你的臉型。

> haircut 則指髮型有做一些幅度的改變，不只是修剪而已。

> hairdo 與 hairstyle 皆指「髮型」。

I'd like to change the color of my hair.

🔊 *Track 189*

我想要改變頭髮的顏色。

▶ Please give me some highlights on the top.
請幫我在上層做些挑染。

▶ I just want to dye the roots of my hair.
我只想染髮根的地方。

▶ I just want to hide my gray hair.
我只想遮蓋白髮。

dye 表示「染色」的意思。這裡也可以用 color，當動詞用。

外國人講「白頭髮」是用 gray hair 灰髮，表示因年紀或黑色素減少而變白的頭髮。

NOTE

穿著服裝

你可以這樣問

💬 **What's the dress code for
tonight's party?**　🔊 *Track 190*

今晚派對的服裝規定是什麼？

▶ We wear business casual on Fridays.
我們星期五可以穿著商務休閒風格的衣服。

你可以這樣說

💬 **These pants are so you.**　🔊 *Track 191*

這條褲子很有你的風格。

▶ You look stylish today.
你今天看起來很時髦。

▶ These jeans are stylish and not expensive.
這條牛仔褲很時髦而且價格不貴。

you 在這裡，表示「你自己的個人風格」。

💬 **I like the way you dress yourself.**　🔊 *Track 192*

我喜歡你穿著打扮的方式。

▶ I never buy the latest fashions.
我從不買最新流行的款式。

▶ You are neatly dressed today.
你今天的穿著看起來乾淨整潔。

▶ You look good in yellow.
你穿黃色很好看。

Chapter 02 著裝

💬 She's fashionably dressed.

Track 193

她打扮得很時尚。

▶ She enjoys dressing up herself.
她很喜歡打扮自己。

---

tacky 這個字就是中文裡形容一個人很 ㄙㄨㄥˊ 的意思。

💬 He's such a sloppy dresser.

Track 194

他的穿著很邋遢。

▶ He's so tacky.
他真是俗。

saggy 有「鬆懈的」、「下垂的」意思，所以「垮褲」是 saggy pants.

▶ I don't like boys wearing saggy pants.
我不喜歡男生穿垮褲。

💬 You look weird in these clothes.

Track 195

你穿這樣看起來很奇怪。

▶ This dress doesn't suit you.
這件洋裝不適合你。

▶ This top is too revealing.
這件上衣太暴露了。

💬 Wearing a miniskirt makes me feel awkward.

Track 196

awkward 可以形容「笨拙、不靈巧」。

穿迷你裙讓我覺得很彆扭。

070

「購衣挑選」

你可以這樣問

💬 **Do you like this kind or that kind?** ◀ *Track 197*

你喜歡這款還是那款？

▶ Which one do you prefer?
你比較喜歡哪一個？

▶ Do you like any of these?
這裡有任何你喜歡的款示嗎？

> kind 款式（名）；
> 仁慈的（形）
>
> prefer 較喜歡，
> 如：I prefer
> coffee to tea.
> 我喜歡咖啡勝
> 於茶。

💬 **Can I try that one on too?** ◀ *Track 198*

我可以也試那件嗎？

▶ Where's the fitting room? 試衣間在哪裡？

▶ You should try them both. 你應該兩件都試穿。

> 「試衣間」亦可
> 使用 dressing
> room。

💬 **How much is this?** ◀ *Track 199*

這個多少錢？

▶ How much does it cost? 這個多少錢？

▶ Is that the best price? 這是最好的價格嗎？

▶ Can you scan the bar code of this sweater for me?
你可以幫我刷一下這件毛衣的價錢嗎？

> best 為 good 的
> 最高級，表示「最
> 好的」。

💬 **Is there anything wrong with the item?** ◀ *Track 200*

這商品有什麼問題呢？

▶ Is there any problem with this jacket?
這件外套有什麼問題嗎？

💬 What is your return policy? ◀ Track 201

你們退換貨的規定是什麼？

policy 政策

▶ Did you check their return policy?
你看過他們的退換貨規定了嗎？

▶ You can return your purchased item within 7 days.
你購買的商品可以在七日內退換。

▶ Damaged goods can't be returned.
損壞的商品是不能退換的。

你可以這樣說

💬 This is a new addition to our line. ◀ Track 202

這是我們的新產品。

brand 亦可解釋為「品牌」。

▶ The new product has just arrived.
這新產品才剛到。

▶ That's brand new. 這是全新的。

💬 It comes in several colors. ◀ Track 203

它有許多顏色。

come in 上市；
come up
開始、發生；
come with
具備

▶ I'll show you some other colors if you want.
如果你想，我可以給你看其它顏色。

▶ There are a few other colors to choose from.
還有其他幾種顏色可以選擇。

💬 It's the latest style. ◀ Track 204

out of date /
old fashion
過時的

這是最新的款式。

▶ It's very fashionable.
那十分的新潮。

stylish 流行的

We can fix the size.

◀ Track 205

我們可以修改尺寸。

▶ **What's your size?** 你的尺吋是？

▶ **It's too tight.** 它太緊了。

▶ **It's a bit loose around the waist.**
它在腰部的地方有點鬆。

> tight 也可以指
> 「勢均力敵的」。
> 如：It was a
> tightgame.
> 它是個勢均力敵
> 的比賽。

I can't make up my mind.

◀ Track 206

我無法做決定。

▶ **It's a hard choice.**
那是個困難的決定。

▶ **It's hard to decide.**
那很難抉擇。

Please help me pick a cool jacket.

◀ Track 207

請幫我挑件不錯的外套。

▶ **What color do you have in mind?**
你對顏色有什麼想法？

▶ **What's your ideal style?**
你理想的款式是？

They have fantastic sales.

◀ Track 208

它們有很棒的折扣。

▶ **Can you give me a discount?**
你可以給我一些折扣嗎？

▶ **Do you offer a cash discount?**
付現金能享有折扣嗎？

> fantastic 極
> 好的，也可用
> great / fabulous
> / awesome /
> amazing / wicked
> 表示。

I'll have to think about it. 　🔊 *Track 209*

我要考慮一下。

▶ I can't afford it. 我負擔不了。

▶ I can't pay that much. 我付不出這麼多。

▶ I'll take this. 我要買這個。

 I'd like to return this. 　🔊 *Track 210*

我想要退還這個。

I'd like = I would like 我想要

▶ Here is my receipt. 這是我的發票。

▶ Did you bring the receipt? 你帶收據來了嗎？

▶ I'll refund your money. 我會把錢退還給你。

 It doesn't fit. 　🔊 *Track 211*

它不合身。

▶ It doesn't seem to work right. 它不合身。

▶ Did you try it on first? 你之前有試穿過嗎？

 I found a tear in the skirt. 　🔊 *Track 212*

我發現裙子上有一個裂痕。

tear（動詞）撕破、扯破，三態為 tear-tore-torn

▶ It arrived damaged. 它到貨時是有損壞的。

▶ There's a stain on here. 這裡有一個污點。

I'm sorry, those items are non-returnable.

對不起,這些商品是不能退的。

Track 213

> non-[…] able
> = not able to
> [...] 如:non-
> returnable = not
> able to return

It says twenty percent off.

上面寫打八折。

▶ Sorry, these are already bargains.
抱歉,這些已經是特價品了。

Track 214

> 241(Two-For-
> One) 即 Buy one
> get one free.
> 皆表示「買一送
> 一」。

> off 可表「去除」,
> 去除 20% 為「打
> 八折」。

NOTE

「性格個性」

你可以這樣說

💬 He is someone you can rely on. ◀ Track 215
他是一個你可以信賴的人。
- ▶ His opinions are trustworthy. 他的意見是可靠的。
- ▶ He is faithful to his friends. 他對朋友很忠實。

💬 You will be happier if you look at the brighter side. ◀ Track 216
如果你往好的一面看，你會高興一點。
- ▶ Try to be optimistic and make yourself a happier person.
  試著樂觀一點，讓自己快樂多一點。
- ▶ I need some constructive suggestions.
  我需要些有建設性的建議。
- ▶ Keep your positive attitude towards life.
  保持你對生命正面積極的態度。

> optimistic「樂觀的」的相反詞是 pessimistic「悲觀的」。

> positive「正面的、積極的」的相反詞是 negative「負面的、消極的」。

💬 Don't be so pessimistic. ◀ Track 217
不要這麼悲觀嘛。
- ▶ Susan is pessimistic about her chances of finding her Mr. Right.
  蘇珊對於要找到真命天子的機率感到悲觀。

💬 He has a strong sense of curiosity for everything. ◀ Track 218
他對於每件事都有強烈的好奇心。

▶ Curiosity kills a cat.
好奇心太強會惹禍上身。

▶ Obviously she has a competitive spirit.
很明顯的，她的好勝心很強。

He's a man with a generous heart. ◀ *Track 219*
他是個心胸寬大的人。

▶ He is very openhanded to his friends.
他對朋友是很豪爽的。

Jimmy pays no attention to details. ◀ *Track 220*
吉米很大而化之。

▶ Don't make a fuss on such details.
不要在這種問題上小題大作。

▶ You should blame your own carelessness.
這要怪你自己粗心大意。

▶ He's a happy-go-lucky person.
他是個隨遇而安的人。

His jokey personality makes him popular among girls. ◀ *Track 221*
他喜歡開玩笑的個性，讓他在女生當中非常吃得開。

He is very confident in himself. ◀ *Track 222*
他很有自信。

▶ She is independent and self-reliant.
她是個獨立自主的人。

Honesty is the best policy.

Track 223

誠實為上策。

▶ Being an honest person is my code of conduct.
當一個誠實的人是我的行為準則。

He has no sense of humor.

Track 224

他完全沒有幽默感。

▶ He's such a humorous person.
他是很有幽默感的人。

▶ I'm in no humor to talk to you right now.
我現在沒心情和你講話。

第三句中的 humor 做「心情」解。

Thank you for being so thoughtful.

Track 225

謝謝你這麼細心。

▶ I appreciate your thoughtfulness.
我非常感激你的體貼。

▶ You should be more thoughtful of your behavior.
你應該要更小心你的行為。

▶ That's very thoughtless of you to do that.
你這麼做是非常有欠考慮的。

thoughtful 的相反詞就是 thoughtless。字尾為 -ful 表示「充滿……、富有……」；字尾為 -less 則表示「缺乏……、不能……」。

She is a woman with charisma.

Track 226

她是位具有迷人領袖氣質的女性。

▶ President Obama is known as a charismatic leader.
歐巴馬總統是一位眾所皆知，具有領袖特質的領導者。

行為態度

Today is my happiest day ever.
Track 227

今天是我有生以來最開心的一天。

It doesn't make any sense.
Track 228

這一點都不合邏輯。

▶ It's not reasonable.
　這是不合理的。

> 「不合理」
> 也可直接用
> unreasonable。

I can't take this anymore.
Track 229

我再也受不了了。

▶ That's enough.
　夠了。

▶ Not again.
　別再來了。

Your support means a lot to me.
Track 230

你的支持對我意義重大。

▶ I don't know how to express my appreciation.
　我不知該如何表達我的感謝。

▶ My gratitude is endless.
　我對你的感激永無止盡。

I feel very uncomfortable with what he said.

Track 231

他說的話讓我很不舒服。

▶ His words pissed me off. 他的話讓我很生氣。

▶ You're getting on my nerves.
你讓我很生氣。

nerve 是「神經」的意思。

▶ His boss makes him see red. 他的老闆讓他很生氣。

I'm a dead man.

Track 232

我完蛋了。

▶ I'm finished. 我完蛋了。

▶ I screwed up. 我搞砸了。

▶ You are doomed. 你完蛋了。

You complete me.

Track 233

我的生命因你而完美。

complete 使完整、使完美

▶ I'm not completed without you.
沒有你，我的生命就不完整。

▶ You light up my life. 你點亮了我的生命。

be (feel) proud of... 為……感到驕傲

I'm so proud of you, my son.

Track 234

兒子，我真以你為榮。

proud 驕傲的；pride 驕傲

▶ We truly feel proud to be your parents.
身為你的父母真讓我們感到驕傲。

a credit 增光的人或事

▶ You're such a credit to our family.
你真是為家族增光的人。

💬 I admire such a versatile person like you.

🔊 *Track 235*

我欽佩像你這樣多才多藝的人。

▶ I admire her literary talent.
我欣賞她的文學天賦。

▶ I admire the way you are.
我欣賞你做人處事的方式。

> admire 佩服、欣賞

> the way you are 表示「你現在的樣子、這樣的你」，可延伸為「做人處事的方式」。

💬 Look before you leap, or you'll regret it.

🔊 *Track 236*

三思而後行，不然你會後悔。

▶ I regret that I gave up too soon.
我後悔我太快放棄了。

▶ I regret what I've done. 我為我所做的事感到後悔。

> regret 後悔、遺憾

> give up 放棄

💬 We're anxious about your safety.

🔊 *Track 237*

我們很擔心你的安全。

▶ I'm anxious about my children's grades.
我很擔心孩子們的成績。

▶ Don't be so anxious about my performance.
別那麼擔心我的表現。

> be anxious about... 為……擔心

💬 I was frightened by the big fire.

🔊 *Track 238*

我被那場大火嚇到了。

▶ I was totally frightened by the earthquake.
我完全被地震嚇到了。

▶ Scary movies always frighten me.
恐怖片永遠讓我感到害怕。

I was embarrassed by your compliments.

🔊 *Track 239*

be embarrassed...
感到尷尬、難為情、窘迫

我對你的恭維感到難為情。

▶ I felt embarrassed when my boyfriend kissed me in public.
我男友當眾親我的時候，我覺得很尷尬。

Shame on you!

🔊 *Track 240*

be (feel) ashamed
感到丟臉

你真丟臉！

shame 羞愧、羞恥、羞怯

▶ Don't you feel ashamed when you tell a lie?
你說謊的時候不覺得丟臉嗎？

▶ I'm ashamed because I flunked English.
我覺得好丟臉，因為我英文被當了。

blush 因害羞而臉紅

▶ I was blushing with shame on the blind date.
我在相親時因為害羞而臉紅了。

NOTE

Part3

讓你輕鬆閒聊的
興趣嗜好會話

「收藏玩味」

你可以這樣問

💬 What kind of food do you prefer? 🔊 *Track 241*

你偏好哪一類食物？

▶ I visit French restaurants frequently.
　我經常造訪法式餐廳。

▶ Mexican food is my favorite.
　墨西哥美食是我的最愛。

- -

你可以這樣說

💬 I'm interested in home decoration. 🔊 *Track 242*

我對居家布置很感興趣。

DIY = do-it-yourself 自己動手製作

▶ I think I have good taste in color schemes, so I paint my house very often.
　我覺得我對配色概念很有品味，所以我很常粉刷家裡。

▶ I tried to remodel my room with some DIY furniture last week.
　我上個月試著用 DIY 家具改造我的房間。

- -

appeal 吸引力、愛好

💬 I am really attracted to gardening. 🔊 *Track 243*

園藝對我非常有吸引力。

gardening 園藝

▶ Gardening on my balcony takes me a lot of time.
　在陽台養花弄草花去我不少時間。

flower pot 盆栽、花盆

▶ I'm satisfied with the flourishing flower pots on my balcony.
　我對陽台茂盛的花草盆栽感到很滿意。

- -

I'm a cat person.
Track 244

我是愛貓人士。

▶ I'm a Persian cat owner.
我養的是波斯貓。

▶ Most pet owners put in a lot of effort to take care of their pets.
大部分養寵物的人都花很多心力照顧寵物。

I'd like to raise a turtle as my pet.
Track 245

我想養隻烏龜當寵物。

▶ Keeping a hamster is a lot of fun.
養倉鼠很好玩。

▶ What do you think of having a snake as a pet?
你覺得養蛇當寵物怎麼樣？

You're such a gourmet.
Track 246

你真是個美食主義者。

▶ You're really an Italian Food epicurean.
你真的是義大利美食專家。

> gourmet /
> gastronomer /
> epicurean 都可表
> 達「美食家、美
> 食主義者」。

I enjoy having great meals in nice restaurants.
Track 247

我喜歡在餐廳享用大餐。

▶ I enjoy delicacies with friends in gourmet restaurants.
我喜歡和朋友在美食餐廳中享用美食。

💬 **You look like you'd be good at wine tasting.** ◀ *Track 248*

你看起來對品酒很在行。

▶ I've learned a lot from a superb wine taster.
   我從一位一流品酒專家那學了不少。

....

💬 **My grandpa has collected antiques for many years.** ◀ *Track 249*

antique(s) 古董;collector 收藏家

我爺爺蒐集古董很多年了。

▶ Go to a flea market, maybe you can find some antiques there.
   也許你能在跳蚤市場找到一些古董。

flea market 跳蚤市場

....

💬 **I heard that you're a souvenir collector.** ◀ *Track 250*

我聽說你是紀念品收藏家。

▶ I've bought about 100 wooden seals as my souvenirs.
   我了大概已經買了一百個木頭章當紀念品了。

「娛樂活動」

你可以這樣問

💬 **What kind of music do you prefer?** ◀ *Track 251*

你喜歡哪種音樂類型?

....

What type of movies do you like? ◀ *Track 252*

你喜歡哪種電影類型？

▶ Comedy is always my first choice.
喜劇片永遠是我的優先選擇。

> genre / type / kind 都為類別、類型；一般電影或音樂分類多使用 genre 這個字。

你可以這樣說

Books are my spiritual inspiration. ◀ *Track 253*

書本是我的精神食糧。

▶ Reading makes me feel fulfilled .
閱讀讓我感到充實。

▶ I feed myself by reading.
我藉閱讀充實自己。

> spiritual / mental 都可表示「精神上的、內在上的」。

> feed myself 餵我自己，可延伸為「自我充實」。

My husband is a bookworm. ◀ *Track 254*

我丈夫是個書蟲。

▶ I'm a bookaholic so I spend a lot of my time in bookstores and libraries.
我是個愛書成癡的人，所以我花許多時間泡在書店和圖書館裡。

> bookworm 書蟲

> -holic 為字尾，表示成癮、成癮，如：bookaholic 愛書成癮者、workaholic 工作狂、alcoholic 酒鬼

I'm crazy about fantasy novels. ◀ *Track 255*

我超迷奇幻小說的。

▶ I'm a super fan of The Twilight Saga .
我是《暮光之城》的超級書迷。

▶ I'm addicted to the Harry Potter series.
我對哈利波特系列小說入迷了。

▶ I was fascinated with scientific fiction when I was ahigh school student.
我高中時超迷科幻小說的。

> fantasy novel 奇幻小說；sci-fi 科幻小說

> be addicted to... / be fascinated with... 對……入迷

💬 I'm very interested in writing poetry.

◀ *Track 256*

我對寫詩很有興趣。

poetry 詩詞的通稱，為集合名詞不可數；poem 詩，一首詩為 a poem；poet 則為「詩人」。

▶ I'd try my best to be a creative poet.
我會努力成為有創造力的詩人。

▶ Some people think that poetry is really hard to understand.
有些人認為詩真的很難懂。

💬 I've spent lots of money and time on movies.

◀ *Track 257*

我花了很多時間、金錢在電影上。

deal with 人「與……相處」

▶ I learned how to deal with my family from family movies.
我從家庭類電影中學會如何與家人相處。

get tired of 對……感到厭煩

▶ I never get tired of Horror films.
我永遠看不膩恐怖片。

💬 I'm a great fan of Rock.

◀ *Track 258*

我是超級搖滾樂迷。

be avid for... 熱衷於……

▶ Many young people are avid for trance music.
很多年輕人熱衷於迷幻樂。

💬 I heard that you have great taste in movies.

◀ *Track 259*

我聽說你很有電影品味。

▶ I prefer artsy and documentary movies.
我比較喜歡藝術類電影和紀錄片。

▶ I always feel sorrow when I watch war movies.
看戰爭片時我總會感到悲傷。

I feel peaceful when I listen to music. ◀ *Track 260*
聽音樂能讓我平靜。

▶ I joined a fanclub of a famous singer.
我參加了一位知名歌手的歌迷俱樂部。

Watching a movie makes me feel ◀ *Track 261*
relaxed.
看電影能讓我放鬆。

▶ It's better to book seats in advance.
最好預先訂位。

> in advance 表示「預先」的意思。

Playing basketball can build up ◀ *Track 262*
team spirit.
打籃球能培養團隊精神。

▶ Let's form a basketball team.
我們組個籃球隊吧！

「球類運動」

你可以這樣說

💬 **Steven is the school basketball team captain.**

◀ *Track 263*

史蒂芬是籃球隊長。

▶ He's a veteran in his basketball team.
他是籃球隊裡的資深球員了。

veteran 老球員、資深球員、老鳥

💬 **Mike is a very nimble shooting guard.**

◀ *Track 264*

麥克是一位相當靈活刁鑽的得分後衛。

point guard / one-guard 控球後衛

shooting guard / two-guard 控球後衛

💬 **The coach gave an order to use the foul strategy.**

◀ *Track 265*

教練下達犯規戰術指令。

▶ After the halftime, the guest team started the one-on-one defense.
中場過後，客場採取盯人防守。

▶ We used the eat-up-the-clock strategy.
我們用連續傳球和運球戰術把比賽時間耗完。

one-on-one defense 盯人防守

eat up the clock / milk the time away 進攻球隊以運球、傳球耗去即將到來的終場結束時間。

💬 **Wilson was trying his best for a box-out.**

◀ *Track 266*

威爾森努力在籃下卡位。

▶ They are the best starting lineup of our basketball team.
他們是我們球隊最佳五人先發。

▶ Although I'm still a bench player, I'm confident that I'll be a starter in the future.
雖然我現在還是板凳球員，但我有信心未來我會成為先發。

starting lineup 先發五人；starter 先發球員

bench player 板凳球員；backup 替補球員

🗨 The point guard winked as a hint for a fast break.
◀ *Track 267*

控球後衛眨眼暗示我們發動快攻。

fast break 快攻

▶ The coach ordered us to adopt the zone defense strategy.
教練指示我們這一節採取區域聯防。

zone defense 區域聯防

▶ What a nice pick-and-roll!
這個擋人切入實在太精采了。

pick and roll 擋人切入戰術

▶ The center got a baseball-pass from his teammate, and suddenly made a slam dunk.
中鋒接到長傳後，突然就灌籃了。

baseball pass 長傳

slam dunk 灌籃

🗨 What the hell! The pitcher made a wild pitch.
◀ *Track 268*

搞什麼！投手投出暴投了。

▶ The catcher made many big mistakes today; he had too many passed-balls.
捕手今天出了大錯，他漏接太多球了。

▶ Great! The catcher used very good pitching tactics today.
太好了！捕手今天的配球很棒！

passed-ball 捕手漏接球；pitching tactics 捕手配球

The left fielder caught that long fly ball. ◀ Track 269

左外野手接殺了那個高飛球。

plate / home base 本壘

▶ The third baseman threw the ball back to the plate without delay,successfully achieving a force out .
三壘手在第一時間將球傳回本壘，成功封殺了跑壘者。

force out 封殺

What a nice double play! ◀ Track 270

真是精彩的雙殺！

double play 雙殺出局

▶ The player is ready to steal the base.
那球員準備要盜壘了。

steal the base 去盜壘；stolen-base 盜壘

My racket is almost worn out. ◀ Track 271

我的球拍差不多要壞了。

All her serves are very powerful. ◀ Track 272

她的發球都很有威力。

serve 發球；service 發球、發球方式

▶ Jack got a bad cold, so his services became much weaker than usual.
傑克重感冒了，所以發球比平常弱許多。

▶ Look! He received the powerful service.
他接住了那個強力發球。

receive 接球

Hank kept slicing balls at his opponent today. ◀ Track 273

漢克今天不斷切球給對手。

▶ His forehand attacks and smashes are very strong.
他的正手拍攻擊和殺球非常強勁。

▶ He scored on a receive error.
他因對方接發球失誤而得分。

slice 切球；
smash 殺球；
forehand attack
正手拍攻擊；
backhand attack
反手拍攻擊

 He struck a drop shot.　◀ *Track 274*

他擊出一個網前吊球。

score 得分；
error 失誤

▶ He served a high clear.
他發了一個高遠球。

▶ He's really good at push shots and net shots.
他非常擅長推搓球和網前球。

strike 擊出球

其他運動

你可以這樣問

 Have you ever tried rock climbing before?　◀ *Track 275*

你曾試過攀岩嗎？

▶ I'm crazy about mountain motorcycle riding.
我超迷騎越野機車的。

sunscreen / UV
cream / sun
block lotion /
sunprotection
lotion 防曬乳
（油）；塗抹防
曬油的動詞可
用 rub / spread /
apply。cream 為
乳狀；lotion 則為
液狀。

How about going swimming at the　◀ *Track 276* **beach next weekend?**

下個週末去海邊游泳怎麼樣？

▶ Remember to rub the sunscreen over your entire
body to protect yourself against UV rays.
記得全身塗上防曬乳來防紫外線！

swimming trunks
男泳褲；bikini 比
基尼；swimsuit
女泳裝

gym / fitness club / sports club / fitness center 都表示「健身房」。club 為「俱樂部」；center 則為「中心」

I'm going to the gym after work. Are you coming along? *Track 277*

我下班後要去健身房，要一起來嗎？

▶ I just registered for the fitness club near our office.
我報名了公司附近的健身中心。

register for / sign up for 報名

▶ I got a big discount because I applied for the yearly membership in this fitness center.
我在這家健身中心申請了年費會員，所以拿到不錯的折扣。

membership 會員、會員資格

Can we train together? *Track 278*

我們可以一起練嗎？

▶ How many sets do you usually do at a time?
你通常一次練幾組？

▶ It's too light for me. Would you add a little more weight for me, please?
這對我來說太輕了。能否請你幫我加點重量？

posture 姿勢

▶ How's my posture? Is it right?
我的姿勢怎麼樣？正確嗎？

你可以這樣說

I'd like to try extreme sports. *Track 279*

我想試試極限運動。

extreme sports / X-Game 極限運動

▶ I challenged myself through extreme sports.
從極限運動中我完成了自我挑戰。

▶ I get closer to the nature from X-Games.
藉著極限運動我更接近大自然了。

💬 I'm taking swimming classes. ◀€ *Track 280*

我正在學游泳。

▶ I've learned to swim in backstroke and freestyle in the past two weeks.
最近兩週我已經學會了自由式和仰式。

> breaststroke 蛙式；front crawl style / freestyle 自由式；backstroke 仰式；sidestroke、dog paddle 狗爬式；butterfly（stroke）蝶式

💬 Swimming is good for your heart and lungs. ◀€ *Track 281*

游泳對心臟及肺部有益。

▶ I did only five laps and I felt worn out.
我才游五圈就筋疲力盡了。

> do a lap 游一圈

> be（feel）worn out 筋疲力盡、累壞了

💬 More and more people enjoy going biking. ◀€ *Track 282*

越來越多人享受騎自行車的樂趣。

▶ I get great pleasure from going biking.
騎腳踏車讓我得到很大的樂趣。

▶ I've joined a biking club and go biking with some new friends in my leisure time.
我參加了一個單車俱樂部，在空閒時就和新朋友去騎單車。

> work out 健身

> leisure time 空閒時間、閒暇

💬 Kick out the kickstand and park your bike here. ◀€ *Track 283*

放下腳架，在這停好你的腳踏車。

▶ There's a bicycle stand here, you can park your bike in.
這裡有個腳踏車架，你可以停進去。

> kickstand 腳架；kick out 可表達「踢下腳架」的動作，收起則為kick up。

> bicycle stand 腳踏車停車架

folding bike
小折；race
bike 公路車；
mountain bike
登山車

My folding bike got a flat tire! ◀ *Track 284*

我的小折爆胎了。

▶ It's not my day today; my bicycle chain slipped when I was riding down from the mountain road.
今天真倒楣，我的腳踏車在我騎下山路時脫鏈了。

got / have
a flat tire 爆
胎；bicycle
chain slip /
have aslipped
bicycle chain
脫鏈

Let's stretch before working out. ◀ *Track 285*

運動前我們先做伸展操吧！

stretch 伸
展、伸展操；
stretch out
伸展開來

I'd like to build my muscles. ◀ *Track 286*

我想鍛鍊肌肉。

▶ How do I make my chest and abs bigger?
怎麼讓胸肌和腹肌變大？

▶ My muscles are sore and aching.
我的肌肉又痠又痛。

work out /
exercise / take
exercise
做運動

NOTE

Part4

讓你不用驚慌的
緊急狀況講法

你可以這樣問

 What can we do when an *Track 287*
earthquake happens?

地震來了怎麼辦？

> 在表示「具體的事物」時，occur 可與 happen 共用。

▶ I hide myself under the table when earthquakes occur.
地震發生時我躲在桌子下面。

▶ Run out of the house if the earthquake is severe.
發生強烈地震時要往屋外跑。

你可以這樣說

 There are many earthquakes in *Track 288*
Taiwan every year.

台灣每年都有很多地震。

▶ Japan also has frequent earthquakes.
日本也經常有地震。

▶ Earthquakes occur frequently along the earthquake zone.
地震帶常有地震。

Most roads are closed due to the *Track 289*
earthquake.

因為地震，大部分道路都被封閉了。

> be blacked out = had a blackout 停電

▶ The traffic is blocked because of the earthquake.
因為地震的關係導致交通大打結。

▶ Taipei City was blacked out because of the sudden earthquake.
突如其來的大地震讓台北市大停電。

The Government of Indonesia issued a tsunami warning.

Track 290

印尼政府發布了海嘯警報。

▶ The frightened tourists on the shore took shelter immediately.
海邊受驚嚇的遊客立刻尋求掩蔽。

tsunami / tidal wave 皆為「海嘯」。

immediately 即時地、立即地

A serious flood affected southern Taiwan this year.

Track 291

台灣南部今年發生了相當大的水災。

▶ Most fields were submerged under the water.
大多數田地被水淹沒了。

▶ Many villages were totally flooded.
許多村莊被完全淹沒了。

The victims are suffering from the pain of losing their family.

Track 292

災民們正遭受失去至親的痛苦。

▶ The flood brought tremendous damages to the disaster area.
這次水災為災區帶來許多意想不到的破壞。

suffer from 受苦、遭受

Stores, schools and train stations were all forced to shut down.

Track 293

商店、學校和火車站全都被迫關閉。

▶ The trains and commuter rail services between Tainan and Kaohsiung were disrupted.
往返於台南至高雄間的火車及通勤列車中斷了。

The traffic is interrupted. = The traffic got stuck. 交通中斷

▶ The traffic between Tainan and Kaohsiung got stuck.
台南至高雄間的交通中斷了。

torrential rain / extremely heavy rain 皆可表示「豪雨」。

It's expected that torrential rain will be brought by the typhoon.

🔊 *Track 294*

這次颱風預計將帶來豪雨。

▶ The torrential rain brought by the typhoon caused mudslides and landslides in the mountain area.
這次颱風帶來的豪雨造成山區土石流和山崩。

mudslide / mudflows 皆可指「土石流」；landslide 則為「山崩」，一般口語亦可表示「土石流」。

The typhoon alert was issued earlier this morning.

🔊 *Track 295*

颱風警報在今天凌晨發佈了。

▶ The Central Weather Bureau issued a sea typhoon warning.
中央氣象局發佈海上颱風警報。

typhoon warning / typhoon alert / an alert for typhoon /a warning for typhoon 皆可表示「颱風警報」。

Hundreds of lives were lost in the severe typhoon.

🔊 *Track 296*

上百人因強颱而失蹤。

▶ Many people were buried under the landslides in the mountain region.
許多人因為山區土石流被活埋。

a sea typhoon alert 海上颱風警報；a land typhoonalert 陸上颱風警報

The drought would affect the harvest this year.

🔊 *Track 297*

乾旱一定會影響今年收成。

▶ The drought will affect the growth of crops.
乾旱將影響農作物生長。

▶ The price of agriculture products keeps going up because of the drought.
農產品價格因為乾旱持續上揚。

The drought caused the shortage of water in southern Taiwan.

◀ *Track 298*

乾旱造成台灣南部缺水。

▶ We should conserve water because the drought is really bad.
我們應該節約用水，因為乾旱真的很嚴重。

▶ The Government announced the temporary water supply cut.
台灣政府宣布暫停供水。

Government 表
「政府」時常以
大寫表達。

Chapter 02 人禍

你可以這樣問

💬 What caused the fire? 🔊 *Track 299*

大火的主因是什麼？

▶ The short circuit caused a big fire in the library.
電線斷路造成圖書館大火。

> burned down
> 指「燒毀、
> 燒得精光」
> 之意。

▶ The gas explosion burned down the factory.
瓦斯氣爆燒光那間工廠。

▶ The bank was burned down by an arsonist.
那個銀行被縱火犯燒得精光。

. . . .

💬 How's the condition of the injury? 🔊 *Track 300*

受傷情況如何？

▶ The mail carrier hit by a car was seriously injured.
那個被車撞的郵差受了重傷。

> become
> disabled 殘廢

▶ She became disabled from the hit-and-run accident.
她因那場肇事逃逸事件而殘廢。

. . . .

你可以這樣說

💬 A big fire broke out near the 🔊 *Track 301*
shopping mall.

購物中心附近發生一場大火。

> break out 為
> 「突然發生、
> 爆發」之意。

▶ A big fire broke out near the night market a couple days ago. 幾天前夜市附近發生了一場大火。

. . . .

💬 Hurry! We must dial 911! 🔊 *Track 302*

快！我們必須打 119！

> be on fire /
> catch fire 皆可
> 表達「著火」
> 或「失火」。

▶ The kitchen is on fire. 廚房起火了。

. . . .

106

The fire detector started beeping five minutes ago. 🔊 *Track 303*

火災警報器五分鐘前開始響了。

▶ The big fire spread very quickly.
大火很快延燒。

• •

I was a witness to the car accident. 🔊 *Track 304*

我是那場車禍的目擊者。

▶ I witnessed the motorcycle accident yesterday.
我昨天目擊那場機車車禍。

▶ My daughter and I saw the pileup in front of the museum with our own eyes.
我女兒和我親眼目睹博物館前那場連環車禍。

witness 當動詞為
「親眼目睹、親
眼所見」；當名
詞可為「目擊者
或見證者」之意。

pileup 連環車禍

• •

She was swimming and had a cramp in her right leg. 🔊 *Track 305*

她在游泳時右腿抽筋了

having a cramp
in + 身體部位＝
身體部位 + be
having acramp
指「正發生抽筋
狀態」。

• •

You'd better watch your wallet all times. 🔊 *Track 306*

你最好隨時注意你的皮夾。

▶ It's easy to have your pockets picked at the night market.
逛夜市時很容易被扒。

• •

💬 **There have been several robbery cases in this area.** ◀ *Track 307*

最近這一帶發生好幾起搶劫事件。

rob 搶劫；robbery 搶劫事件；robber 搶匪

▶ A convenient store was robbed at late night.
一家便利商店在深夜被搶了。

▶ The bank robber escaped with a great sum of money and shot a security guard.
銀行搶匪帶走鉅款逃跑，而且射殺了一位保全人員。

💬 **A thief sneaked into my house and stole all my jewelry last night.** ◀ *Track 308*

小偷昨晚溜進我家，偷走我所有珠寶。

▶ I saw him stealing my necklace and sneaking it into his pocket.
我看到他偷我的項鍊，然後塞進他口袋裡。

homeless 無家可歸的人，表「流浪漢」之意。

💬 **My brother was attacked by a homeless person last night.** ◀ *Track 309*

我弟昨晚被流浪漢攻擊了。

assault 為「施暴、毆打」之意。

▶ The poor wife has been assaulted by her alcoholic husband for at least one year.
那可憐的妻子被她酗酒的丈夫施暴至少一年。

💬 **That was definitely a fraud call.** ◀ *Track 310*

那絕對是詐騙電話！

harass 騷擾；sexual harassment 性騷擾

▶ I don't think it was a fraud call, just a harassing call.
我想那不是電話詐騙，只是一通騷擾電話。

💬 **That guy is a fraud.**

🔊 *Track 311*

那傢伙是個騙子。

▶ I can't believe such a smart person like him would be swindled by a fraud clan.
像他這麼聰明的人竟會被詐騙集團給騙了。

> fraud clan / fraudulent organization / a ring of swindlers 皆可表示「詐騙集團」。

NOTE

Part 5

讓你快速融入的
學校職場會話

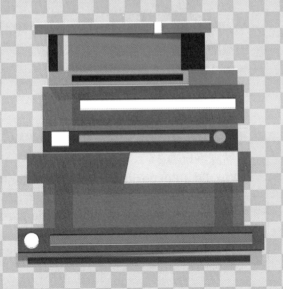

「校園學習」

你可以這樣問

favorite 最喜愛的（形容詞）；最愛（名詞）

🗨 **What's your favorite subject?** ◀ *Track 312*

你最喜歡的科目是什麼？

▶ I like geography the most. 我最喜歡地理。

🗨 **Did anything happen at school today?** ◀ *Track 313*

今天學校裡有發生什麼事嗎？

class leader 班長；transfer (student) 轉學生

▶ I was chosen to be the class leader.
我被選為班長了。

▶ There's a transfer student in our class.
我們班上來了一個轉學生。

homework / assignment 作業、回家功課

🗨 **What does a class leader have to do?** ◀ *Track 314*

班長應該要做些什麼呢？

call the roll 點名；roll-call time 點名時間

▶ Call the roll every morning.
每天早上點名。

science 自然科

🗨 **Is your science class interesting?** ◀ *Track 315*

自然課好玩嗎？

▶ We did an experiment on light reflection.
我們做了一個光線折射的實驗。

do (have) an experiment 做實驗

▶ We went to a park to observe the plants.
我們去公園觀察植物。

specimen 標本

▶ Teacher showed us lots of insect specimens.
老師展示好多昆蟲標本。

When's your mid-term exam?

Track 316

你的期中考是什麼時候？

> mid-term exam
> 期中考；final
> exam 期末考

▶ I'll have my mid-term exam two weeks later.
兩個禮拜後就是期中考了。

▶ The final exam is coming and I'm very nervous about it.
期末考快到了，我好緊張。

> review 複習

Did you take any notes in math class today?

Track 317

你今天在數學課有寫筆記嗎？

> take notes 表示
> 「記筆記」的
> 意思。

▶ Do you often take notes during class?
在課堂上時你常寫筆記嗎？

你可以這樣說

I forgot to bring my homework to school today.

Track 318

我今天忘了帶作業到學校了。

▶ I didn't have enough time to finish my homework.
我時間不夠，功課做不完。

▶ My teacher punished me to make copies of the new lesson twice.
老師罰我罰抄新課文兩次。

> make a copy /
> make copies
> 抄寫

We are going to discuss our school work this evening. ◀ *Track 319*

我們今天晚上要討論功課。

assign 指「指派」的意思。

▶ Our group will use the projector and computer to support our oral presentation today.
我們的組別今天會使用投影機和電腦來做口頭報告。

▶ Our group found some reference sources to our assignment.
我們組別找到一些報告的參考資料。

highlight 是「強調、使……顯著」的意思。

I have highlighted some important points in the textbook. ◀ *Track 320*

我在課本裡面有標重點。

I have to study English grammar for tomorrow's quiz. ◀ *Track 321*

我必須準備明天的文法考試。

announce 是「宣佈」的意思。

▶ The teacher will announce the date of the geography exam for this class.
老師將會公佈地理考試的日期。

▶ The math exam will be held next Monday, the 11th of January.
數學考試將在下週一一月十一號舉行。

I have to finish reading my part before the group discussion. ◀ *Track 322*

分組討論前我要讀完我的部份。

▶ Before group discussions I always browse in advance what has to be read.
在分組討論前我都會先瀏覽過應該閱讀的部份。

> browse 是指「瀏覽」的意思。

💬 **Our group has some questions to discuss about this chapter.**　◀ *Track 323*
我們組對這章節有些問題。

▶ I have some questions to ask the teacher regarding the chemistry book.
我有些化學課本的問題要問老師。

> regarding... 表示「關於……」的意思。

升學進修

你可以這樣問

💬 **What major do you want to study in the future?**　◀ *Track 324*
你以後想唸什麼科系？

▶ I plan to study in graduate school after college.
我計畫唸完大學後讀研究所。

💬 **Is there an age limit for getting the certificate?**　◀ *Track 325*
拿這個證照有年紀限制嗎？

▶ How long does this course take for students to qualify for a certificate?
要花多久的課程時間來拿到證照資格？

▶ My certificate is issued by the government.
我的證照是政府發行的。

> issue 指「核發」的意思。

How do I enroll in a school?

◀ *Track 326*

placement exam 指「學生分班考試」的意思。

如何申請入學？

▶ This placement exam is very important to me.
這個分班考試對我來説很重要。

How much is the application fee for this school?

◀ *Track 327*

application fee 指「申請費用」的意思。

申請這間學校要繳多少錢？

What do I need to apply for school loans?

◀ *Track 328*

loans 指「貸款」的意思。

申請助學貸款需要什麼？

financial statement 指「財力證明」的意思。

▶ I need to have a financial statement to apply for that school.
我要提供財力證明來申請那間學校。

▶ How much is the tuition fee (book fee)?
學費／書籍費要多少錢？

Are there any dorms at the school?

◀ *Track 329*

boarding school 指「提供寄宿的學校」。

學校裡有宿舍嗎？

▶ Is this a boarding school?
這是一間寄宿學校嗎？

你可以這樣說

It is never too late to learn.

◀ *Track 330*

學習永不嫌晚。

▶ Education can enrich your life.
教育可以豐富你的生命。

take exam 是「考試」的意思。

▶ What are the dates for taking the college entrance exam?
大學入學考試是哪幾天？

enrich 是「充實」的意思。

I need to buy some more reference books to study. ◀ Track 331
我需要買一些參考書來讀。

reference book 表示「參考書」的意思。

Having more professional training is ◀ Track 332 a way to survive in the job market.
接受在職進修是一個能夠在職場生存的方法。

▶ The most popular programs for continuing education would be for items that are on demand on the job market now.
最受歡迎的推廣教育課程都是現在職場上最有需求的工作項目。

on demand 需求

I'm certified in hair designing. ◀ Track 333
我有美髮設計的認證。

acquire 指「取得」的意思。

▶ I have acquired a certificate in pet grooming.
我獲得了寵物美容師認證。

pet groomer 指「寵物美容師」的意思。

▶ Do you need any certification or a license to be a dog groomer?
你需要任何認證或執照來當狗兒美容師嗎？

license 是「執照、許可證」的意思。

The placement exam will be held on next Monday.
🔊 Track 334

分班測驗將於下週一舉行。

> hold an exam 表示「舉辦考試」的意思。

School will begin soon.
🔊 Track 335

學校快開學了。

▶ Summer vacation will end soon. 暑假快接近尾聲了。

▶ How many days left before school begins?
還有幾天要開學了？

You will get a student identification number.
🔊 Track 336

你會得到一個學生證號碼。

> enroll 在此表示「註冊、登記」的意思。

▶ You will get a student identification number when you enroll at the school.
當你到學校註冊時，你會得到一個學生證號碼。

> swipe 在此表示「滑動」的意思。

▶ You can swipe your student identification card to enter the school library.
你可以用你的學生證刷卡進入學校圖書館。

多元學習

你可以這樣問

How about taking taekwondo classes?
🔊 Track 337

> taekwondo 跆拳道；karate 空手道

考慮一下去上跆拳道課如何？

What kind of instrument do you want to learn?

🔊 *Track 338*

你想學什麼樂器呢？

▶ Cool! Learning to play the piano is a good choice.
很棒！學彈鋼琴是好選擇。

▶ How about going to percussion music classes?
去上打擊樂課怎麼樣？

> instrument 樂器；piano 鋼琴；violin 小提琴；percussion music 打擊樂

> 彈奏樂器使用的動詞為 play。

你可以這樣說

I think you should go to a cram school.

🔊 *Track 339*

我想你應該去補習班上課。

▶ Your math has become rusty. 你的數學變糟了。

> rusty 糟、荒廢

I'm planning to take you to the museum.

🔊 *Track 340*

我正計畫帶你去博物館。

Working holidays is a way to experience local cultures deeply.

🔊 *Track 341*

打工渡假是深刻體驗當地文化的方法。

▶ You will need a working holiday visa to travel and work abroad.
當你到國外工作和旅行時你需要一個打工渡假簽證。

> local 指「當地」的意思。

▶ Choosing homestay is a great way to experience a different culture.
選擇當地住宿是個體驗不同文化的一種方法。

> homestay 指「在當地居民家居住」。

💬 Come join our club!

🔊 *Track 342*

加入我們的社團吧！

▶ Have you joined any club yet? 你有加入社團嗎？

▶ Do you have any favorite clubs you want to join?
你有想要加入的社團嗎？

club 可當作
「俱樂部」或
「學校社團」
的意思。

💬 I take dance classes on weekends.

🔊 *Track 343*

週末時我有參加舞蹈課程。

▶ Do you know any information on dancing courses on weekends?
你知道任何參加週末舞蹈課程的資訊嗎？

💬 I like to learn many languages.

🔊 *Track 344*

我喜歡學習很多種語言。

▶ I can not only speak Chinese but also Japanese.
我不只會講中文還會說日文。

▶ My French teacher can speak more than 10 languages.
我的法文老師會說超過十種語言。

not only...
but also 指
「不僅……
也會……」的
意思。

💬 Frankly speaking, distance teaching is effective for me.

🔊 *Track 345*

坦白說，遠距教學對我來說挺有效的。

▶ Generally speaking, distance teaching is very popular abroad.
一般而言，在國外遠距教學非常受歡迎。

▶ Honestly speaking, distance teaching makes me feel sleepy.
老實說，遠距教學讓我昏昏欲睡。

打工求職

你可以這樣說

💬 **I want a summer job during my** ◀┊ *Track 346*
school break.

我暑假想要打工。

▶ Where can I find a job listing?
哪裡可以找到工作欄？

> break 在此指
> 「休息、暫停」
> 的意思。

💬 **You can also be a tutor at night.** ◀┊ *Track 347*

晚上你也可以兼職家教。

▶ I have to babysit every night to make some money.
我必須每晚當保母賺些零用錢。

▶ I work as a teacher's assistant when I have free
time in the school.
在學校我一有空閒時間就當教師助理。

> babysit 在此當動
> 詞，表示「臨時
> 保母」的意思。

💬 **You can post your resume online.** ◀┊ *Track 348*

你可以上網刊登你的履歷。

▶ You can read some part-time job ads on the school
newspaper every week.
每個禮拜你都可以在學校報紙上看到一些打工徵職的廣告。

> post 在此表示
> 「刊登文章」的
> 意思。

▶ There are a lot of job opportunities for you to
choose from if you know how to find them.
如果你知道方法，你可以找到很多工作機會。

> opportunity 在此
> 表示「機會」的
> 意思。

This part-time job suits my school hours.
Track 349

這個打工適合我的學校時間。

▶ The job is paid by hour, not by month.
這個工作是時薪制而不是月薪制。

▶ The owner of this bookstore offers a reasonable salary for part-time workers.
這個書店的老闆提供打工者合理的工資。

> suit 在此當動詞，表示「適合」的意思。

日常業務

你可以這樣問

What time is the meeting?
Track 350

會議是從幾點開始？

▶ How long do you think the meeting will be?
你覺得會議要開多久？

▶ Is the meeting going to last for two hours?
會議會持續兩小時嗎？

> last 在這裡是當「持續」解釋。

What's today's agenda?
Track 351

今天的議程是什麼？

▶ What's on the agenda? 議程有哪些？

Who's taking the minutes?
Track 352

誰要做會議紀錄？

▶ Who will keep the minutes? 誰要負責做紀錄？

> minute 是「分鐘」，在這裡當「會議紀錄」的意思。

Would you walk me through the workflow?

◀ *Track 353*

可以麻煩你跟我講一下工作流程嗎？

・・・・・・・・・・・・・・・・・・・・・・・・・・・・・・・・・・・・・・

What are your standard procedures?

◀ *Track 354*

你們的標準程序是什麼？

▶ Please follow the procedures.
請依照程序來。

▶ I'm going to establish a procedure for this.
我會建立一個程序。

> 這裡的 establish 也可以用 set up 來替換。

・・・・・・・・・・・・・・・・・・・・・・・・・・・・・・・・・・・・・・

你可以這樣說

I'll be in meetings all day today.

◀ *Track 355*

我今天有一整天的會。

▶ I have three meetings in a row.
我有連續三個會議要開。

・・・・・・・・・・・・・・・・・・・・・・・・・・・・・・・・・・・・・・

The meeting is going to be rescheduled.

◀ *Track 356*

會議必須要重新安排時間。

▶ The meeting will be postponed.
會議要延遲舉行。

▶ Let's postpone the meeting until this afternoon.
會議延到下午再開。

▶ The meeting is cancelled. 會議取消了。

> postpone 與 delay 都有「延遲」的意思。postpone 表示「將原先預定好時間的事情延緩辦理」，delay 則是「將預定要在時限內完成的事情，因為某些不好的原因無法完成而必須延長期限辦理」。

・・・・・・・・・・・・・・・・・・・・・・・・・・・・・・・・・・・・・・

I will set up a time for a meeting. 🔊 *Track 357*

我會來安排一個會議時間。

▶ Please set up a meeting right away to clarify the currentsituation.
請立即安排一個會議來釐清一下目前的狀況。

▶ We should have a reviewing meeting.
我們應該來開個檢討會議。

I've just been given a new assignment. 🔊 *Track 358*

我剛被指派新的工作。

▶ How come I'm always given emergency assignments?
為何我總是被指派緊急任務？

This pie chart shows that our sales 🔊 *Track 359* income represents sixty percent of the total income.

這個圓餅圖顯示我們的業績收入占全公司的 **60%**。

pie chart 圓餅圖；bar chart 條狀圖；flow chart 流程圖；line chart 曲線圖；organization chart 組織圖

▶ I have no idea what this chart indicates.
我不知道這張圖表代表的意義是什麼。

▶ I think you should create another chart to clarify your points.
我覺得你需要製作另一張圖表來闡明你的論點。

I'm running late on my sales report. 🔊 *Track 360*

我的業績報告要來不及了。

▶ I have a report to turn in this afternoon.
我今天下午要交一個報告。

▶ The monthly report is due this Friday.
本週五前要交月報告。

💬 **I want to revise this plan.**   ◀ *Track 361*

我要修改一下這個計畫。

▶ The head office will probably terminate this plan.
總公司大概會終止這個計畫。

▶ We have been told to proceed with the plan.
我們被告知要繼續執行這個計畫。

💬 **We are running a sales promotion**   ◀ *Track 362*
to achieve the sales target.

我們正在實施一個促銷案以達到業績目標。

▶ I haven't reached my sales quota yet.
我還沒有達到我的銷貨配額。

▶ Our department's sales have exceeded the target by 150 percent.
我們部門的營業額已經超出目標 150%。

▶ After a difficult period, we are finally in the black.
經過了一段艱辛的日子以後，我們終於有盈餘了。

> in the black 表示「有盈餘」，表示在財務報表上不再有紅字。相反的，in the red 就表示仍在「虧損、負債」。

💬 **Our goal is to increase our market**   ◀ *Track 363*
share.

我們的目標是要增加市場佔有率。

▶ We will have new products next year to expand our market share.
我們明年會增加產品以擴大市場佔有率。

▶ It is a necessity to run some marketing campaigns to maintain the market share.
執行一些市場行銷活動以維持市場佔有率是必要的。

「職場協調」

你可以這樣問

💬 **Excess me. Where is the copy machine?**　◀ *Track 364*

請問影印機在哪裡呢？

▶ Can you show me where the HR is?
可以麻煩你告訴我人力資源部在哪裡嗎？

▶ Where do you keep the files?
請問檔案都放在哪裡？

「人力資源部」的英文是 Human Resources，常簡稱為HR。

- -

💬 **Is it ok if I use a personal day this Friday?**　◀ *Track 365*

請問我本週五可以請假嗎？

▶ Will it be ok if I take the last week of October off?
我可以十月的最後一週休假嗎？

- -

💬 **Could you reconsider this?**　◀ *Track 366*

針對這件事你可以再做考慮嗎？

▶ Please think it over. 請再思考一下。

- -

💬 **Do you mind helping me with something?**　◀ *Track 367*

你介不介意幫我一個忙？

▶ Can you do me a favor? 你可以幫我一個忙嗎？

▶ Could you help me out? 可以請你幫忙一下嗎？

▶ Would you please give me a hand?
可以請你幫忙一下嗎？

How's your schedule today?

Track 368

你今天的行程如何？

▶ I have a tight schedule this week.
我這星期的行程很滿。

▶ I'm completely tied up today.
我今天的時間已經被佔滿了。

> tight 是形容「緊繃的」，形容時間或空間時，意思為「滿的、緊湊的」意思。

你可以這樣說

This is our new colleague.

Track 369

這是我們的新同事。

▶ Mark is going to be part of our team starting from today.
馬克從今天開始是我們團隊的一份子。

▶ Let's welcome Mark to our company!
讓我們歡迎馬克加入我們公司！

Let me introduce you to our workplace.

Track 370

讓我為你介紹我們的工作環境。

▶ Here is the conference room.
這裡是會議室。

▶ We have a tea break at three thirty.
我們在三點半有個午茶時間。

Please let me know if I'm doing anything wrong.

Track 371

如果我做錯了請告訴我。

▶ Please don't hesitate to correct me if I'm doing anything wrong.
如果我做錯了，請不用遲疑馬上指正我。

I'm sorry that I'll be twenty minutes late today.

Track 372

很抱歉我要晚進來二十分鐘。

▶ I'm sorry for being late. 對不起，我遲到了。

▶ I apologize for being late. 我為我的遲到道歉。

I have to use a sick day today.

Track 373

我今天必須要請病假。

▶ I have a fever and I won't be able to come in today.
我正在發燒，今天沒有辦法進辦公室。

▶ I feel terrible and I can't make it to the office.
我很不舒服，沒有辦法進公司。

I have some personal urgent matters to deal with.

Track 374

我有一些私人緊急事件要處理。

I understand your point of view.

Track 375

我了解你的觀點。

▶ I understand what you're talking about.
我了解你在說什麼。

▶ I see your concern. 我懂你在意的點。

> concern 表示「關心、在意的事」。

I agree with you on that point.

🔊 Track 376

關於這點，我同意你的看法。

▶ I'll only accept under certain conditions.
我只有在特定條件下同意。

▶ I would agree but with qualifications.
我可以有條件的同意。

> 左述兩句，都是代表有條件的同意，都附帶了其他的但書。

We can be flexible over this.

🔊 Track 377

關於這點我們有討論的空間。

▶ I can make some concessions.
我可以做些讓步。

> flexible 是個常用的形容詞，表示人或事是「彈性的、可商量的」。

Please get to the point.

🔊 Track 378

麻煩您說重點。

▶ Would you stick to the point? 您可以只說重點嗎？

▶ Let's get back to the main issue. 讓我們回到正題。

▶ What are you trying to say? 你的重點是什麼？

Let's wrap up the discussion.

🔊 Track 379

我們來為這次討論做個總結吧。

▶ We need to go over some details first.
我們要先討論一些細節。

▶ Let's take a vote on this matter.
針對本案我們來作投票表決。

💬 That seems like a reasonable offer. 🔊 *Track 380*

這提議不錯。

▶ I'm afraid this is the best we could do.
我們能做到的就是這樣了。

▶ It's a deal.
就這麼說定了。

‥‥‥‥‥‥‥‥‥‥‥‥‥‥‥‥‥‥‥‥‥‥‥‥‥‥‥‥‥‥‥

💬 Let's get it straight. 🔊 *Track 381*

我們來把事情講清楚。

▶ Let's not give each other a hard time.
我們別跟彼此過不去。

‥‥‥‥‥‥‥‥‥‥‥‥‥‥‥‥‥‥‥‥‥‥‥‥‥‥‥‥‥‥‥

💬 Next Friday will be my last day. 🔊 *Track 382*

下週五是我最後一天上班。

▶ I'm leaving the company.
我要離開這間公司了。

「親朋好友」

你可以這樣問

How many people are there in your family?

◀ *Track 383*

你家有幾個人？

▶ Do you have a big family or a small family?
你家是個大家族還是小家庭？

▶ Is your family a nuclear family?
你家是小家庭嗎？

> nuclear family 表示「小家庭，只包括父母和子女」的意思。

What are you going to do on the weekend?

◀ *Track 384*

你週末要做什麼？

▶ Do you have any plans for the weekend?
你週末有任何計畫嗎？

What have you been doing lately?

◀ *Track 385*

你最近在忙什麼？

▶ What are you up to?
最近在忙什麼？

▶ Where have you been lately?
最近你跑到哪裡去啦？

▶ What's new with you?
近來有什麼新消息嗎？

▶ What's up?
近來有什麼新鮮事嗎？

> What's up? 為口語用法，也可用於問人「怎麼啦？」或「發生什麼事？」

When should I give you a call?

Track 386

give a ring 及 give a call 為口語用法，表示「打電話」的意思。

我何時方便打電話給你？

▶ When is a convenient time to reach you?
什麼時候方便找你？

Are we going shopping now?

Track 387

我們要去逛街嗎？

▶ We should come to this restaurant more often.
我們應該常來這家餐廳。

▶ I like the atmosphere here.
我喜歡這裡的氣氛。

你可以這樣說

My mom and I look alike.

Track 388

我媽跟我長得很像。

▶ My father and my brother look like each other.
我爸和我哥長得一模一樣。

▶ My sister and I are totally different.
我和我妹長得一點也不像。

My brother and I are very close.

Track 389

我跟我弟弟感情很好。

▶ My grandma and I have a lot in common.
我奶奶和我有很多共通點。

get along with 表示「相處融洽」的意思。

▶ I get along with my cousin.
我和表姊相處很融洽。

My family and I are going on a vacation to Paris.

Track 390

我們全家要到巴黎度假。

▶ We will have a family trip to Japan.
我們全家將去日本旅遊。

I get along well with my mother-in-law.

Track 391

我跟我婆婆相處得很好。

▶ My in-laws are coming to visit us this weekend.
我的公婆週末要來看我們。

in-law 表示是因「法律」而成為親人，就是「姻親」；in-laws 可指公婆或丈人 / 丈母娘。

in-law 為複合名詞，複數型為 in-laws。

We are looking forward to the birth of the baby.

Track 392

我們正在期待新生兒的來臨。

▶ The baby is due in two weeks.
小孩再兩星期就要出生了。

due 當形容詞是「到期的」意思，例：The report is duethis Friday. 報告這星期五到期。也就是「本週五要交報告的意思。」due date 則有「寶寶到期的日子」，也就是「預產期」。

The baby has arrived.

Track 393

孩子出生了。

▶ Congratulations on your sweet little delivery.
恭喜你喜獲麟兒。

I care about you.

Track 394

我很關心你。

▶ I am the one who cares.
我很關心你。

care about 在
此表示「關
心」的意思。

▶ I'll be there for you.
我會在你身邊守護著你。

▶ I don't care.
我不在乎。

「常規禮儀」

你可以這樣說

🗨 **Swallow before you talk please.** ◀ *Track 395*

請吞下食物後再講話。

▶ It's rude to talk with your mouth full.
滿口食物講話是很沒禮貌的。

🗨 **Please watch your table manners,** ◀ *Track 396*

kids.

table manners
餐桌禮儀

孩子們,請注意你們的餐桌禮儀。

🗨 **Catch you later.** ◀ *Track 397*

此句雖有 later
等一下,但即
使不是待會見
也可以用來
道別。

再見。

▶ See you around.
再見。

▶ See ya.
再見。

ya 是 you 的口
語用法。

▶ Later.
再見。

That's why.

◀ *Track 398*

原來是這樣。

▶ Now I see.
現在我了解了。

▶ Gotcha.
我懂你的意思了。

see 有「看」的意思，但此句意指「了解」。

Gotcha. 有兩種意思，一種是 I've got you. 意為「我抓到你了。」。另一種涵義為「I get it.」也就是 I get what you're talkingabout.「我知道你在說什麼了。」的意思。

Go break a leg.

◀ *Track 399*

祝你好運。

▶ Good luck.
祝你好運。

▶ Bless you.
上帝保祐你。

I blew it.

◀ *Track 400*

我搞砸了。

▶ I screwed it up. 我搞砸了。

▶ I messed it up. 我搞砸了。

Go break a leg. 這是一句「反話」，常用在他人正準備上場表演或比賽時，給予的祝福語。

It's up to you.

◀ *Track 401*

你決定。

▶ It's your call. 你決定。

They invited me to John's party tonight.

◀ *Track 402*

他們邀請我參加約翰今晚辦的派對。

▶ Are you coming?
你要來嗎？

party animal
是指「很愛
參加派對的
人」。這種人
在派對上常有
瘋狂的舉動，
戲稱為 party
animal。

welcome
party 歡迎派
對；barbecue
party 烤肉
派對。

BYOB 最早的使
用是 Bring Your
Own Bag 請自
備環保袋，後來
在國外有許多派
對，主人會事先
告知 BYOB，延
伸為 Bring Your
Own Bottle 的意
思，也就是主人
不主動提供酒精
飲料，賓客請自
備。末尾的 B 可
替換成不同的意
思，例 BBQ 派
對的 BYOB 可
表示 Bring Your
OwnBeef，或
Bring Your Own
Beer。

▶ Who else will go?
還有誰會去？

▶ He's a party animal.
他是個派對狂。

Don't stand me up.
◀ Track 403

別放我鴿子。

▶ I was stood up.
我被放鴿子了。

▶ Be on time.
請準時。

It's a farewell party.
◀ Track 404

那是一個歡送派對。

▶ It's a BYOB party.
這是一個「請自備酒瓶」的派對。

We had a great time.
◀ Track 405

我們玩得很愉快。

▶ Have a nice trip. 祝旅途愉快。

溝通交流

你可以這樣問

Does anyone have any additional remarks?
◀ Track 406

還有沒有補充意見？

▶ Does anyone have different opinions?
有沒有人有不同看法？

additional remark
表示「補充說明」
的意思。

▶ Please seize the final opportunity.
請把握最後的機會。

seize 表示「把握」的意思。

 Do you approve? ◀ *Track 407*

你同意嗎？

▶ Have you made up your mind?
你決定了嗎？

 你可以這樣說

 **Eye contact is very important** ◀ *Track 408*
when you talk.

說話時，眼神接觸非常重要。

▶ I advise you to listen to your children's heart, not just listen to what they say.
我建議你聽聽孩子們的心裡話，別僅只是聽他們講的話。

Let's think it over. ◀ *Track 409*

讓我們仔細考慮。

▶ Don't rush into making decisions. 不要急著做決定。

rush into 是「倉促行事」的意思。

I would like to speak. ◀ *Track 410*

我要求發言。

▶ Please allow me to say something.
讓我說一下。

ask for 是「要求」的意思。

▶ I have some suggestions. 我有一些建議。

137

Please speak up.
◀ *Track 411*

請大家踴躍發言。

▶ We really need to collect suggestions from all of you.
我們真的很需要蒐集大家的意見。

collect from 表示「蒐集」的意思。

I think what you just said is right.
◀ *Track 412*

我覺得你說的很對。

▶ I agree with your claim.
我同意你的主張。

▶ I identify with your viewpoint.
我認同你的意見。

identify with 表示「認同」的意思。

We must discuss this matter all over again.
◀ *Track 413*

我們得重新討論這件事。

▶ The original method doesn't work.
原來的方法行不通。

▶ Do we have any new strategies?
有沒有新的策略？

Do not deliver a speech with anger.
◀ *Track 414*

發表意見不要有情緒。

▶ Please talk calmly.
冷靜一點說。

▶ Don't lose your temper.
不要發脾氣！

deliver a speech 表示「發表演說」的意思。

We should listen to others.
 🔊 *Track 415*

我們應該要聽別人的意見。

▶ Maybe we'll get some different points of view from others.
或許我們可以得到其他人不同的看法。

> point of view 表示「看法」的意思。

Your request is unreasonable.
 🔊 *Track 416*

你的要求太過份了！

▶ Don't ask too much. 不要要求太多！

▶ I'm not going to say yes to all of these.
我不可能答應這麼多。

> reasonable 表示「合理」的意思；相反詞是 unreasonable「不合理」。

NOTE

Part6

讓你跟上潮流的
現代新知講法

Chapter 01 投資理財

「投資規劃」

你可以這樣問

What was the total volume of the stock market today?
◀ *Track 417*

今天股市總成交量如何？

▶ Was the close good today?
今天收盤價好嗎？

> 股票被套牢的動詞，可用 trap。

▶ All my money was trapped in the stock market.
我的錢都在股市裡套牢了。

- -

How much are your mutual funds profits?
◀ *Track 418*

你的基金獲利多少？

▶ I expect my return from long-term investing in mutual funds.
我期待投資基金的長期回收。

- -

> per 每

How much is the international gold price per ounce?
◀ *Track 419*

> USD 美元，念法為 US dollars。

國際金價每盎司多少錢？

▶ Some investors even predict the gold price will reach up to US$2000.
有些投資人甚至預測金價將會上升至 2000 美元。

> reach 達到

- -

Have you ever thought of making some foreign currency investments?

Track 420

你曾想過進行外幣投資嗎？

▶ Is foreign currency investment highly profitable?
外幣是高獲利投資嗎？

currency 貨幣；foreign currency 外幣

profitable 獲利的、有利的

你可以這樣說

risk 風險；risky 有風險的

Investing in stocks is risky.

Track 421

投資股票是有風險的。

▶ I guess I can't handle the risk of investing in stocks.
我想我不能忍受股票投資的風險。

▶ Can you handle the risk of stock trading?
你能承受股票交易的風險嗎？

the stock goes up 股票上升；the stock goes down 股票下跌

This stock is a blue chip.

Track 422

這股票是支績優股。

▶ I raked a lot of money from stock investments last year.
我去年在股票投資上賺了一大筆。

chip 是指「籌碼」的意思，blue chip 則通常是指「價值最高的籌碼」，在這裡表示證券市場價值最高的股票，稱為「藍籌股」。人們把股票市場上實力雄厚、活躍的股票稱為「藍籌股」。

All the stocks I invested in reached their limit yesterday.

Track 423

我投資的股票昨天全漲停板了。

▶ My dad reads the tape carefully every day.
我爸每天都仔細看盤。

rake 指「很快賺得錢財」。

limit up 漲停板；limit down 跌停板

read the tape 看盤

You can look for a professional mutual funds manager for investment consultation.

🔊 *Track 424*

你可以找位專業基金經理人提供投資諮詢。

consult 諮詢；
consultant 顧問；
consultation 諮商、諮詢

▶ He can figure out the advantages of mutual funds for you. 他可以為你指點基金獲利。

▶ A professional mutual funds manager would analyze the disadvantages and risks for his clients immediately.
專業的基金經理人立即會為客戶分析基金損失與風險。

Investing in mutual funds is also a good method of financial investment.

🔊 *Track 425*

conservative
保守的

買基金也是投資理財的好方法。

mutual fund /
managed fund
都可表示「基金」。

▶ Mutual funds investment is more conservative than stocks investment.
基金投資比股票投資來得保守些。

The apartments in safe neighborhoods are very expensive.

🔊 *Track 426*

位於較安全的社區的公寓非常昂貴。

▶ I can't afford anapartment in a good neighborhood because the price is too fancy.
我負擔不起高安全性社區的公寓，價格實在太高了。

down payment
頭期款

I have finally saved enough money for the down payment on my own studio.

🔊 *Track 427*

我終於存夠我的套房頭期款了。

▶ I am going to apply for a home purchase loan.
我要去申請購屋貸款。

home purchase loan 購屋貸款

My mom wants to invest in real estate and be a landlord after her retirement.

◀ *Track 428*

我媽想投資房地產，在退休後當個公寓房東。

studio 套房；apartment 公寓；condominium 華廈；duplex 雙併屋；house 獨棟房屋

▶ I think I have to take out a loan to buy this condominium.
我想我得貸款來買這棟華廈。

儲蓄保險

你可以這樣問

What's the interest rate on a checking account?

◀ *Track 429*

活期帳戶利率大概多少？

current deposit / demand deposit / current account / checking account 活存

▶ The interest rate of current accounts is getting lower and lower.
活存利息變得越來越低。

How much bank savings are there in your account?

◀ *Track 430*

你的帳戶裡有多少存款？

bank saving / bank deposit 存款

▶ I spend almost all my income every month, so I don't have any savings.
我每個月幾乎都花光薪水，所以我沒有任何存款。

beneficiary
受益人

insurance
policy 保單

risk
declaration
form 風險告
知書

Who's the beneficiary of the insurance policy?

◀ *Track 431*

誰是這張保單的受益人？

▶ Would you please provide a risk declaration form?
能否請你提供我風險告知書？

你可以這樣說

fixed deposit
/ time deposit
/ savings
account 定存

make a
deposit 存錢

I feel like opening an additional demand deposit.

◀ *Track 432*

我想多開個定存帳戶。

▶ I made up my mind to make a deposit into a savings account.
我決定把錢存進定存帳戶。

save / deposit
存

I'm planning to save five thousand dollars in my account every month.

◀ *Track 433*

我打算每個月存五千塊到我的帳戶。

I'd like to open an installment savings account for insurance.

◀ *Track 434*

我想為保險開個零存整付帳戶。

▶ What papers should I prepare for opening a new account?
我開新帳戶需要準備什麼證件？

Saving your money in a bank is reliable.

◀ *Track 435*

把錢存在銀行裡是可靠的。

▶ I feel secure depositing money in a bank.
把錢存進銀行讓我感到安心。

reliable 可靠的、可信賴的

secure 安全的、放心的

Jane is a senior insurance personnel.

◀ *Track 436*

珍是位資深保險員。

insurance personnel / insurance agent / insurance broker 保險員

I'm going to buy medical insurance.

◀ *Track 437*

我想買份醫療保險。

▶ Do not terminate your husband's accident insurance because his job is highly risky.
別解約你老公的意外險，因為他的工作具有高度風險。

insurance agency / insurer / insurance company 保險公司

terminate 終止（動詞）；termination 終止（名詞）

Labor insurance is very important for all of us.

◀ *Track 438*

勞保對我們所有人來說是非常重要的。

▶ The finances of the National Health Insurance has been in the red for many years.
全民健保財務虧損好幾年了。

labor insurance、worker's insurance 勞保；National Health Insurance 全民健保；National Pension Insurance 國民年金

be in the red / be in debt 虧損、負債

「數位資訊」

你可以這樣問

How do I subscribe to international roaming services for my cell phone? ◀ *Track 439*

我要怎麼申請手機國際漫遊服務？

▶ The international roaming service makes me feel carefree while traveling overseas.
國際漫遊服務讓我出國旅遊時更輕鬆。

你可以這樣說

My computer crashed. ◀ *Track 440*

我的電腦當機了。

▶ My computer is down.
我的電腦當機了。

▶ Look! The screen is frozen.
看！螢幕動也不動。

You have to reinstall the O.S. ◀ *Track 441*

你的電腦必須重灌作業系統。

▶ How do I uninstall this program?
如何移除這個程式？

un- 字首之單字表示「相反、否定」之意；uninstall 為「移除」之意。

Your computer has got a virus. ◀ *Track 442*

你的電腦中毒了。

▶ My computer is infected.
我的電腦中毒了。

▶ My PC was attacked by the malware.
我的桌上型電腦被惡意軟體攻擊了。

▶ Anti-Spyware and firewalls are also important for protecting our computers.
防間諜軟體和防火牆對保護電腦安全也很重要。

> anti- 在字首表示
「反……、對抗」
之意。

I'd like to burn three CDs. 　🔊 *Track 443*

我想燒三片光碟。

▶ I don't know how to duplicate CDs.
我不知道怎麼複製光碟。

> CD burner 光碟
燒錄機；burn a
CD 燒光碟

This picture looks so shaky. 　🔊 *Track 444*

這張照片看起來好模糊。

▶ Is this picture over-exposed? 這張照片是不是過度曝光了？

▶ Most photos we took today look under-exposed.
今天拍的大部分照片看起來都曝光不足。

> look ＋形容詞「看
起來……」

You really have a camera face! 　🔊 *Track 445*

你真的很上相！

▶ Hey! The camera loves you. 嘿！你真的蠻上相的！

▶ I think you look better in person.
我覺得你本人比照片好看喔！

The connection doesn't seem to 　🔊 *Track 446*
be good nearby.

這附近訊號似乎不太好。

> seem 看來、似乎

▶ Have you lost your signal, too? 你也收不到訊號嗎？

▶ I can't hear what you're saying. 我聽不到你在講什麼。

My screen has some scratches.

◀ Track 447

我的螢幕有刮痕。

▶ The key pad doesn't work well so I can't send text messages.
按鍵接觸不良,所以我不能傳簡訊。

▶ It will take about seven to ten workings days to fix it.
送修約需七到十日。

get lost = be lost 迷路

The GPS helps me to no longer get lost.

◀ Track 448

衛星導航讓我再也不會迷路。

GPS = global positioning system 全球衛星定位系統

▶ I've never been lost since I bought a GPS.
買了 GPS 後,我再也沒迷路過了。

網際網路

你可以這樣問

Did you save my blog address as your Favorite?

◀ Track 449

你把我的部落格網址加入我的最愛了嗎?

get online 上網

▶ There were some connection problems with my computer, so I couldn't get online yesterday.
昨天我的電腦有些連線問題,所以我昨天不能上網。

Have you signed up for Facebook yet?

🔊 *Track 450*

你註冊臉書帳號了嗎？

▶ I unfriended Mike on Facebook.
我刪除跟麥克的臉書好友關係了。

unfriend 是社交網站下的產物，其意義為「將某人從臉書的朋友名單上刪除」，表示切斷與這個人的聯繫。在這裡當做動詞來用。

Which shopping website do you surf the most?

🔊 *Track 451*

你最常瀏覽哪個購物網站？

▶ Girls always enjoy surfing on web stores.
女生總喜歡在網路商店上瀏覽。

你可以這樣說

I can't access that website.

🔊 *Track 452*

我無法連上那個網站。

▶ I'd like to search for some health-related information on the Internet.
我想在網路上找些健康相關資訊。

▶ All you have to do is to key in the keyword in the search bar on search engines.
你只需在搜尋引擎的搜索欄位輸入關鍵字即可。

I hate email spam very much.

🔊 *Track 453*

我超討厭垃圾郵件的。

▶ What can I do to block the pop-ups?
我要怎麼樣才能攔截彈出視窗？

▶ Google it! You'll get a solution.
Google 一下，你就能找到方法。

His messenger status is "away".

🔊 *Track 454*

他的聊天程式狀態是「離開」。

．．．．．．．．．．．．．．．．．．．．．．．．．．．．

Don't bother me, or I'll block you.

🔊 *Track 455*

別煩我，否則我就封鎖你。

．．．．．．．．．．．．．．．．．．．．．．．．．．．．

I didn't mean to ignore your messages last night.

🔊 *Track 456*

我昨晚不是故意不回你訊息的。

．．．．．．．．．．．．．．．．．．．．．．．．．．．．

blog 為 web log 的縮寫，為個人網路日誌之意，在台灣通稱為部落格。

I just created a blog to share my daily thoughts and photos.

🔊 *Track 457*

我才剛申請一個部落格來分享我每天的想法和照片。

▶ I'm ready to be a popular blogger.
　我準備好當個人氣部落客了。

blogger 為部落格使用者，在台灣通稱為部落客。

．．．．．．．．．．．．．．．．．．．．．．．．．．．．

3C 產品為 Communication 「通訊」、Computer 「電腦」和 Consumer「消費性」等產品。

Online shopping is very common nowadays.

🔊 *Track 458*

現今的網路購物非常普及。

．．．．．．．．．．．．．．．．．．．．．．．．．．．．

地形景觀

你可以這樣說

Mount Vesuvius in Italy is an active volcano.

◀ Track 459

義大利的維蘇威火山是一座活火山。

▶ What about Mt. Fuji in Japan?
　那日本的富士山呢？

▶ That is a dormant volcano.
　那是座休眠火山。

Generally, there would be hot springs near volcanoes.

◀ Track 460

通常，火山附近會有溫泉。

▶ I visit Yangmingshan to take a hot spring bath every winter.
　每年冬天我都會上陽明山泡湯。

hot spring 溫泉

take a hot spring bath / bathe in the hot spring / dip in the hot spring / soak in the hot spring 泡溫泉

There might be a volcanic activity from the active volcano.

◀ Track 461

這座活火山可能會有火山活動。

▶ All areas near the active volcano are not allowed to be entered.
　這座活火山附近所有區域都禁止進入。

▶ All areas around the active volcano are closed.
　這座活火山附近的所有區域都被封鎖了。

volcanic activity 火山活動

volcanic 當形容詞表示「火山的」，或「由火山所構成的」。

I enjoy looking at the coast from the top of the mountain.

Track 462

我喜歡從山頂眺望海岸。

overlook 眺望

▶ I missed the days when I could gaze at the sea from thebeach resort.
我懷念從海邊度假中心看海的日子。

resort 度假中心、度假處所或度假名勝；villa 別墅

▶ I'm dreaming of living in a houseoverlooking the sea.
我夢想住在可以看海的房子。

The scenery of the coastline around Taiwan is very beautiful.

Track 463

coast 沿岸；rocky coast 岩岸；coastline 海岸線；coastal 沿岸的

台灣的海岸線風景非常美麗。

▶ Taitung County is famous for its rocky coast.
台東縣以岩岸聞名。

issue 議題、問題

The ocean pollution has become an important environmental issue in recent years.

Track 464

海洋汙染是近幾年來重要的環境議題。

ocean 和 sea 都是「海洋」之意，差別在於 ocean 所指的面積範圍較大，偏向中文的「洋」，如大西洋、太平洋；而 sea 則可泛指一般我們所稱的「海」。

▶ Keeping the beach clean is everyone's responsibility.
保持海灘乾淨人人有責。

▶ Never leave garbage on the beach.
千萬別留任何垃圾在沙灘。

I enjoy breathing the fresh air in the mountains.

Track 465

我喜歡呼吸山裡清新的空氣。

▶ I always feel totally relaxed when I walk into the green woods.
當我走進青翠的森林中，我總感到輕鬆無比。

The mountain areas look cloudy and foggy in early mornings.
◀ *Track 466*

清晨時，山區看起來佈滿雲霧。

▶ Don't worry, there's just a little mist in the hills.
別擔心，山上只有一點薄霧。

> cloudy 多雲的；
> foggy 多霧的；
> cloud 雲；fog 霧

The temperature in the mountain areas is lower.
◀ *Track 467*

山區溫度較低。

▶ The atmosphere is lower in the mountains.
高山上氣壓較低。

▶ The air in the mountains is thick so we would find it hard to breathe.
高山空氣稀薄所以我們會覺得呼吸困難。

> temperature 溫
> 度；atmosphere
> 氣壓

The rushing roaring waterfalls look so spectacular.
◀ *Track 468*

湍急的瀑布看起來好壯觀。

▶ The rushing waterfalls took our breath away.
湍急的瀑布讓我們驚嘆不已。

> take one's breath
> away 讓人屏息，
> 意指「使人驚
> 嘆」。

The flowers are coming out little by little.

◀≶ *Track 469*

flowers come out 花朵綻放、開花

花兒正慢慢綻放。

▶ Spring has come and the cherry blossoms have come out.
春天來到，櫻花已經綻放。

hemisphere 半球；the northern hemisphere 北半球；
the southern hemisphere 南半球

Emperor Penguins come from the southern hemisphere.

◀≶ *Track 470*

國王企鵝來自南半球。

▶ The South Pole is the coldest place in the world.
南極是全世界最寒冷的地方。

the South Pole 南極

生態綠能

你可以這樣問

Is the condition of global warming critical?

◀≶ *Track 471*

critical 危急的、要緊的、關鍵性的

全球暖化情況危急嗎？

▶ How serious is the situation of global warming?
全球暖化情況有多嚴重？

What else can we do for energy conservation?

◀≶ *Track 472*

我們還能為節省能源做些什麼？

▶ Any good ideas for energy saving and carbon reduction?
關於節能減碳還有其他好想法嗎？

▶ Anything else?
還有其他的嗎？

saving 和 conservation 為「節省」的名詞。

What are the benefits of organic fruits and vegetables?

◀ *Track 473*

有機蔬果的益處是什麼？

▶ Is eating organic fruit and vegetables beneficial for anti-aging and my skin?
如果吃有機蔬果，是不是對抗老化和肌膚有好處？

benefit 益處、好處；beneficial 有益處的

anti-aging 抗老化

你可以這樣說

Animal conservation is a very important and urgent matter.

◀ *Track 474*

動物保育是重要而緊急的。

▶ Don't buy furs and eat wild animals.
不要買皮草和吃野生動物。

fur 皮草；
wild animals 野生動物

Never abandon your pets.

◀ *Track 475*

絕對不要棄養你的寵物。

▶ How about adopting a stray dog instead of buying one?
以認養流浪狗取代購買怎麼樣？

stray dog 流浪狗；
stray animals 流浪動物

The Arctic ice is melting faster than expected.

Track 476

北極融冰速度增快超乎預期。

▶ More and more disasters are caused by the global warming effect.
越來越多天災是由地球暖化所造成。

Arctic 北極的、北極圈的（形容詞）；北極地帶（名詞）

The changes of the global climate look unusual.

Track 477

全球氣候變化看起來不尋常。

▶ The Greenhouse effect makes the temperature on earth keep going up year by year.
溫室效應造成地球溫度逐年持續上升。

The water pollution seriously affects the ecological balance.

Track 478

河川汙染嚴重影響生態平衡。

ecological balance 生態平衡

waste 廢棄物

▶ Too much waste from factories poured into the rivers, somany rivers were polluted.
太多來自工廠的廢棄物傾倒入河裡，所以許多河川被汙染了。

river renovation 河川整治

▶ The result of the renovation of Love River in Kaohsiung is really successful.
高雄愛河的整治結果真的非常成功。

I have no idea how to sort the garbage.

Track 479

我不清楚怎麼將這些垃圾進行分類。

進行垃圾分類的動詞為 sort。

▶ Centralize unusable copies and newspapers in the wastepaper collection place.
將印壞的廢紙和報紙集中在廢紙收集處。

wastepaper 廢紙

. . . .

Please collect these PET bottles and aluminum cans.

◀ Track 480

請收集這些鋁罐和保特瓶。

PET bottle 和 plastic bottle 都可表示「寶特瓶」；plastic 則為「塑膠」。

▶ Don't forget to recycle beverage packs.
別忘了回收鋁箔包。

beverage pack 鋁箔包

. . . .

Glass and metal materials are also recyclable.

◀ Track 481

玻璃和金屬物質也是可回收的。

▶ I suggest you to re-use all plastic bags.
我建議你重複使用所有塑膠袋。

canvas 帆布；canvas bag 帆布袋；canvas shopping bag 環保購物袋

▶ Bring a canvas shopping bag with you while you go shopping.
去逛街時帶著環保購物袋吧！

. . . .

The concept of energy saving and carbon reduction is getting popular.

◀ Track 482

節能減碳的概念越來越受歡迎。

. . . .

The animal habitats are on the decrease.

Track 483

desertification
沙漠化；
desert 沙漠

deforestation
森林砍伐

動物棲息地變得越來越少。

▶ The fast melting of Arctic ice is bringing a serious threat to polar bears.
快速北極融冰對北極熊是很大的威脅。

▶ Desertification is the result of deforestation.
土地沙漠化是森林濫伐的結果。

Scientists have warned that more and more animals are on the verge of extinction.

Track 484

extinction 絕
種、滅種

endangered
species 瀕臨
絕種動物；
species 物種

科學家警告越來越多動物正瀕臨絕種。

▶ Seahorses have become an endangered species.
海馬已經變成瀕臨絕種動物。

Green Architectures provide you an energy-saving home.

Track 485

綠建築提供你一個節能居家。

▶ Your house can help the earth save energy as well.
你的房子也能幫助地球節省能源。

「未來科技」

你可以這樣問

What does nanometer mean?
◀ Track 486

奈米是什麼意思？

▶ May I beg your pardon?
抱歉，可以請你再說一次嗎？

▶ Pardon? I've never heard of the term before.
什麼？我從沒聽過這個詞。

nanometer 奈米

Is it the latest technology?
◀ Track 487

它是最新科技嗎？

▶ Not really. 不算是。

▶ I heard that Nanotechnology can be used in many ways.
我聽說奈米科技可以有許多應用方法。

latest 最新的

Nanotechnology
奈米科技

Are there any connections between nanotech and our daily life?
◀ Track 488

奈米科技和我們的日常生活有其他連結嗎？

▶ Nanotech has been applied to home appliances.
奈米科技已經實行在家電用品上。

connection
聯結、關聯

Can you imagine how science and technology will develop in the future?
◀ Track 489

你能想像未來科技將如何發展嗎？

▶ I guess scientists would make "impossible" possible.
我想科學家會把不可能變成可能。

imagine 想像
（動詞）；
imagination 想
像、幻想、異想
（名詞）

come true 使
成真；dreams
come true 夢
想成真

▶ We will make our imagination come true someday.
   總有一天我們會讓想像成真。

What can a robot do for us in the future?

Track 490

機器人將來可以為我們做什麼？

▶ I guess all housework will be done by robots.
   我猜所有家事都會讓機器人來處理。

How will e-books improve?

Track 491

電子書將會如何改良？

▶ E-book readers will be in trend in this decade.
   電子書在未來的十年內會蔚為潮流。

▶ You can scan contents of your book or magazine into your reader in a few seconds.
   你可以在幾秒內將書本或雜誌內容掃描進閱讀器。

你可以這樣說

Nanotech is used a lot in the medical and biological field.

Track 492

field 領域

奈米科技大量運用於醫學和生物科技領域上。

be put to use
in... 應用於
……

▶ Nanotech is also put to use in biotechnology to develop more biomaterials.
   奈米科技也應用於生物科技上，以發展更多生物材料。

Nanotech will be used for killing cancer cells in the future.

◀️ *Track 493*

奈米科技未來可被用於殺死癌細胞。

▶ It might be used for the diagnosis of cancer in the future.
它未來可能被用來診斷癌症。

cancer 癌症；
cancer cells
癌細胞

tissue 組織

- -

Nanotech can help washing machines remove musty smells.

◀️ *Track 494*

奈米科技可以幫助洗衣機去除異味。

▶ Clothes produced with nanotech can reflect, block and absorb UV.
奈米製成的衣物可以折射、阻擋和吸收紫外線。

musty 黴菌的；
musty smell
霉味；must 黴、
發霉

- -

Biotech integrated with agriculture assist farmers a lot.

◀️ *Track 495*

生物科技和農業結合對農夫幫助不少。

▶ Some genetically-modified plants grow faster or look different.
一些基因改造植物會生長較快或者長得不太一樣。

▶ Soybeans and tomatoes are common genetically-modified food.
大豆和番茄是一般常見的基因改造食品。

integrate with
(into)... 結合、
融合

biotech 生物科
技；agriculture
農業

genetic-modified
food 基因改造
食品

- -

The achievement of biotech applied to nutriments is remarkable.

◀️ *Track 496*

生物科技在營養補充品的應用上有傑出的成績。

nutriment / health
food / dietary
supplement food
保健食品、營養
補充品

- -

I wish the screen will be as thin as paper in the future.

◀ *Track 497*

我希望螢幕有一天會像紙一樣薄。

as... as... 像
……一樣

▶ Maybe we would be able to fold a screen as small as we want.
也許有一天我們可以把螢幕折成我們想要的大小。

a roll of 一捲

▶ That would be fun. Maybe we'll buy a roll of screen in shops in the future.
真好玩。也許未來我們將在店裡買到一捲螢幕。

星際奧秘

你可以這樣問

exist 存在
（動詞）；
existence 存
在（名詞）

Do aliens really exist?

◀ *Track 498*

外星人真的存在嗎？

as far as I
know... 據我
所知

▶ As far as I know, the existence of aliens is possible.
據我所知，外星人的存在是可能的。

Have you ever seen a solar eclipse before?

◀ *Track 499*

你看過日蝕嗎？

total solar
eclipse 日全
蝕；partial
solar eclipse
日偏蝕

▶ This will be my first time to observe a solar eclipse, and I'm so excited!
這將會是我第一次看到日蝕，我超興奮的。

你可以這樣說

Other planets rotate around the sun. ◀︎ *Track 500*

其他星球繞著太陽運轉。

▶ Can you name the eight planets of the solar system?
  你能說出太陽系八大行星的名字嗎？

> rotate 運轉（動詞）；rotation 運轉（名詞）

I heard that the environment on Mars is similar to that on Earth. ◀︎ *Track 501*

我聽說火星和地球環境相似。

▶ The surface of Mars looks reddish, so it's also called "the red planet."
  火星表面看起來是淡紅色的，所以也被叫做「紅色星球」。

My younger brother is a big fan of astronomy. ◀︎ *Track 502*

我弟是個超級天文迷。

▶ He knows a lot about meteors and comets.
  他知道很多關於流星和彗星的事。

▶ He told me a long story about why Pluto has become a dwarf planet.
  他告訴我許多關於冥王星變成矮行星的故事。

> dwarf planet 次於行星一級的稱為「矮行星」。

> tell a long story 說了一個很長的故事，意指「說了許多或詳細說明」。

My son dreams of becoming an astronaut or astronomer in the future. ◀︎ *Track 503*

我兒子夢想將來能成為太空人或天文學家。

> Astronomy 天文學；astronaut 太空人；astronomer 天文學家

There are thousands of stars in the Galaxy. ◀ *Track 504*

銀河系中有成千上萬的星體。

the Galaxy /
the Milky Way
Galaxy 都可指
「銀河系」。

▶ The Solar System is located in the Milky Way Galaxy.
太陽系位於銀河系中。

simply 僅僅、
只是

▶ The Solar System is simply one of the stars.
太陽系只是這些星體其中之一。

Astronauts take spacecrafts to explore the outer space. ◀ *Track 505*

太空人乘著太空船在外太空探險。

▶ Many fans of UFOs believe that the aliens take UFOs to our planet.
許多幽浮迷相信太空人乘著幽浮來到地球。

▶ Some people believe that the Crop Circles are made by aliens.
有些人相信麥田圈是外星人造成的。

There are still more galaxies beyond the Galaxy. ◀ *Track 506*

還有更多銀河系在這個銀河系之外。

spaceship
太空船

▶ The day will come when people can take a spaceship to other planets.
總有一天，人們將能乘著太空船到其他星球。

The sun rises from the east. ◀ *Track 507*

太陽從東邊升起。

▶ **The sun sets earlier in winter.**
太陽在冬天比較早落下。

> sunrise 日出；
> sunset 日落

▶ **It's really romantic to see sunsets at the beach.**
在海邊看日落很浪漫。

The moon is blocked by the clouds. ◀ *Track 508*
月亮被雲層遮住了。

> full moon 滿月；
> first quarter of
> the moon 上弦。

▶ **We're going to enjoy the full moon at Sun-Moon Lake on the Mid-Autumn Festival.**
我們準備在中秋節去日月潭賞月。

> the moon at
> the last (third)
> quarter = an old
> moon 下弦月

I saw a lunar eclipse last Sunday. ◀ *Track 509*
我在上週日看到月蝕。

> telescope 望遠鏡

▶ **Sam brought a telescope to observe a lunar eclipse in Yangmingshan.**
山姆帶了一台望遠鏡去陽明山觀察月蝕。

> observe 觀察

> lunar eclipse
> 月蝕

We're ready to watch the stars. ◀ *Track 510*
我們準備好去看星星了。

▶ **The myriads of glittery stars twinkle in the sky.**
天空閃爍著點點璀璨繁星。

> myriad 大量；
> 大量的

▶ **Can you recognize any star signs in a starry night?**
在繁星點點的夜空中，你能認出任何星座嗎？

> twinkle 星星閃
> 爍、發光

Part 7

讓你沒有壓力的
旅遊度假會話

旅遊計畫

你可以這樣問

name 一般是當名詞，表示「姓名、名稱」。在這裡是當動詞，表示「為……命名、列舉」的意思。

Where do you want to go?
🔊 *Track 511*

你想去哪裡？

▶ **Any ideas?** 有什麼想法？

▶ **Name** me some places. 隨便說幾個地點。

What do you think about a beach holiday?
🔊 *Track 512*

你覺得去海島度假如何？

要詢問他人意願時，可以用 How about... 做開頭。

▶ **How about** a shopping holiday? 來個血拼之旅怎樣？

Is Paris worth visiting?
🔊 *Track 513*

巴黎值得去嗎？

▶ What's there to see in Paris? 巴黎有什麼好看的？

How much is the 10-day tour to Canada?
🔊 *Track 514*

加拿大十日遊團費多少？

▶ How much does it cost for each person?
每個人團費多少？

How many people are there in the group?
🔊 *Track 515*

一團有幾個人？

▶ How many people altogether? 總共有多少人？

Can we have a discount?
Track 516

能不能打折啊？

▶ **Any discounts?** 有沒有折扣？

▶ **Is it cheaper for four?** 四人同行有沒有便宜一點？

Is there a Chinese-speaking guide?
Track 517

有說中文的導遊嗎？

▶ **Does our leader speak good English?**
我們的領隊英文好嗎？

Can I pay with a credit card?
Track 518

可以用信用卡付團費嗎？

▶ **I don't have enough cash.** 我現金帶得不夠。

▶ **I can transfer the fee to your account.**
我可以用轉帳付費。

Who should I talk to if I have any problems?
Track 519

我有問題可以找誰？

▶ **Who can help me with problems?** 有問題誰能幫我？

What's the fare for economy class to New York?
Track 520

去紐約的經濟艙票價多少？

▶ **How much is the business class fare to Toronto?**
去多倫多的商務艙票價多少？

▶ How much is the first class fare to Paris?
去巴黎的頭等艙票價多少？

Is there any direct flight?
🔊 *Track 521*

有直飛的班機嗎？

▶ All direct flights are full.
所有直飛的班機都客滿了。

Can I use my miles to upgrade my seat?
🔊 *Track 522*

可以用累積哩程升等座位嗎？

▶ What can I do with my current miles?
我現有的哩程可以用來幹嘛？

What do I need?
🔊 *Track 523*

我需要什麼？

▶ What do I need to prepare?
我需要準備什麼？

▶ What do I need to have with me?
我需要攜帶什麼東西？

Do I need a visa for Germany?
🔊 *Track 524*

去德國要簽證嗎？

▶ I want to apply for a single entry visa.
我想辦單次入境簽證。

▶ She needs a multiple-entry visa.
她需要多次入境簽證。

Where can I apply for a landing visa?

◀ *Track 525*

我要到哪裡辦落地簽證？

▶ I already have a visa.
我已經有簽證了。

▶ I didn't know I need a visa.
我不知道需要辦簽證。

Will five days be enough for New York?

◀ *Track 526*

去紐約五天夠嗎？

▶ How many days do I need for Kyoto?
去京都應該要玩幾天？

▶ How much time should I spend in Barcelona?
在巴塞隆那要待多久？

Do I need an adapter?

◀ *Track 527*

需要帶轉接插頭嗎？

▶ What kind of adapter do I need for New Zealand?
去紐西蘭要用哪一種轉接插頭？

What's the voltage in Australia?

◀ *Track 528*

澳洲的電壓多少？

▶ I'm not sure about the voltage in Japan.
我不確定日本的電壓是多少。

▶ I'll look up the voltage in the U.K.
我會查一下英國的電壓。

look up 表示「查詢」的意思。

down 除了常
見表示「向下
的、在下方」
的意思，在這
裡是當名詞，
表示「羽絨」
的意思。

Should I bring my down jacket?

🔊 *Track 529*

我該不該帶羽絨外套呢？

▶ I'm going to bring my gloves.
我會帶手套。

▶ I'll take my scarf with me. 我會帶圍巾。

你可以這樣說

I want to go skiing.

🔊 *Track 530*

我想去滑雪。

be dying for /
to 表示「極為
想要」的
意思。

▶ She is dying to go to Egypt. 她超想去埃及。

Five days is too short.

🔊 *Track 531*

五天太短了啦。

▶ Can we make the trip longer?
可不可以把行程拉長？

▶ Can we make the trip shorter?
可不可以把行程縮短？

My budget is limited.

🔊 *Track 532*

我的預算不多。

I want to try backpacking.

🔊 *Track 533*

我想試著當背包客。

▶ I'd like to be a backpacker. 我想當背包客看看。

▶ I want to go without joining a tour group.
我不想跟團。

It's easier to go with a tour group. ◀ *Track 534*
還是跟團比較簡單。
▶ It's more convenient to join a tour group.
跟團比較方便。
▶ Joining a tour group saves us trouble.
跟團省麻煩。

save someone trouble 表示「省麻煩」的意思。

All of the package tours are fully booked. ◀ *Track 535*
所有的套裝行程都額滿了。
▶ There are no more seats. 沒有名額了。

book 當名詞時表示「書本、冊子」，在這裡是當動詞，表示「預約、訂位」的意思。

package tour 即為「套裝行程」。

The visa fee is excluded. ◀ *Track 536*
團費不包括簽證費。
▶ The insurance fee is extra. 保險費要另外付。

There are four of us. ◀ *Track 537*
我們有四個人。
▶ I'd like to book for two adults and two kids.
我要報名兩大兩小。

I'd like 是 I would like 的縮寫與口語用法，表示禮貌性的請求。

I'll fax my passport copy to you. ◀ *Track 538*
我把護照影本傳真過去。
▶ I'll fax you my passport copy.
我把護照印本傳給你。
▶ Please fax me the itinerary. 請把行程傳給我。

fax ＋某物＋ to ＋某人，表示傳真某物給某人的意思；而替代用法 fax ＋某人＋某物時，不需加 to。

I'd like to book a flight to New York. ◀ Track 539

我想訂去紐約的機位。

▶ I'd like to reserve a seat to New York.
我要訂一個去紐約的位子。

I made the reservation in Taipei. ◀ Track 540

我在台北訂位的。

▶ I booked my flight through my agent.
我是透過旅行社業務訂位的。

round trip ticket 和 return ticket 皆表示「來回票」的意思，後者乃英式英語常見說法。

I'd like to book a one-way ticket. ◀ Track 541

我要訂單程票。

▶ I'd like a round trip ticket.
我要訂來回票。

My reservation number is AZ6768. ◀ Track 542

我的訂位號碼是 **AZ6768**。

▶ My reference number is MK3535.
訂位代號是 MK3535。

▶ I have a reservation number, it is WA5000.
我有訂位號碼，是 WA5000。

I'd like to reconfirm my flight. ◀ Track 543

我要再確認我的班機。

▶ I'm calling to reconfirm my flight.
我打電話來再次確認班機。

I need to book for special meals. ◀ *Track 544*

我需要訂特殊餐點。

▶ I'm a vegetarian. 我吃奶蛋素。

▶ I'm a vegan. 我吃全素。

> vegan 為不吃魚、肉、蛋、乳製品的嚴格「素食者」。

I need to apply for a new passport. ◀ *Track 545*

我必須申請新的護照。

▶ His old passport is damaged.
他的舊護照毀損了。

> apply for 表示「申請（工作、學校、證件）」的意思。

I want to have my passport photo taken. ◀ *Track 546*

我要照大頭照。

▶ I need a photo taken for my passport.
我需要辦護照用的照片。

▶ Please take my passport photo.
請幫我照大頭照。

I won't be able to come pick it up. ◀ *Track 547*

我沒辦法來取件。

▶ I can't come for it. 我沒辦法來拿。

▶ Can I have it delivered? 可以用快遞的嗎？

Here is my bank statement. ◀ *Track 548*

這是我的財力證明。

▶ Here is the copy of my passbook. 這是我的存簿影本。

> 存摺的說法除了 passbook，還有 bankbook 和 depositbook。

I want to apply for a tourist visa.
◀ Track 549

我想申請觀光簽證。

▶ She needs to apply for a student visa.
她需要申請學生簽證。

▶ He got a working holiday visa.
他拿到打工度假簽證。

▶ You need a business visa for your business trip.
你去出差需要辦商務簽證。

I want to find out the average temperature.
◀ Track 550

我想知道平均氣溫。

▶ What's the temperature now?
現在溫度大概多少？

▶ What's the weather like?
現在天氣怎麼樣？

find out 表示
「查明、找出」
的意思。

Let's get a map first.
◀ Track 551

先買一張地圖吧。

▶ Where can I get a map of Berlin?
哪裡買得到柏林的地圖？

▶ Do you have any London maps?
你們有賣倫敦的地圖嗎？

▶ Is the city map for free?
市區地圖是免費的嗎？

We should take one domestic flight to save time.
◀ Track 552

我們應該搭一段國內線節省時間。

▶ Taking the bus can save us money.
搭巴士可以省錢。

▶ Taking the train is more comfortable.
搭火車比較舒適。

domestic 表示
「國內的」，相
對於 international
「國際的」。

We should take malaria pills.

◀ *Track 553*

我們應該吃瘧疾預防藥。

▶ She already received the prevention shot.
她已經接受了預防注射。

take pills /
medicine 表示
「服用藥物」的
意思。

It's too dangerous to travel in Nepal now.

◀ *Track 554*

現在去尼泊爾太危險了。

▶ Sudan is also under red alert.
蘇丹目前也處於紅色警戒。

under red alert 表
示「處於紅色警
戒狀態」，即為
最危險的警示。

Don't forget the mosquito repellent.

◀ *Track 555*

別忘了帶防蚊液。

▶ Remember to bring your guide book.
記得要帶旅遊指南。

I'll bring my cell phone for roaming.

◀ *Track 556*

我會帶手機使用漫遊。

▶ I'll get a local SIM card.
我會在當地買一張 SIM 卡。

Make sure you have your passport and ticket with you. ◀ *Track 557*

記得要帶護照和機票。

I can't fit my stuff in the suitcase. ◀ *Track 558*

我的行李裝不下了。

fit in 表示「裝入、塞下」的意思。

▶ I got too much stuff.
  我的東西太多了。

▶ There is no more space in my suitcase.
  我的行李箱沒位子了。

你可以這樣問

Can I get a window seat?

Track 559

我要靠窗的位子。

▶ Can I get an aisle seat?

我可以要靠走道的位子嗎？

▶ I'd like to sit next to my friend.

我想坐在我朋友旁邊。

在機場辦理登機手續時，航空公司人員會詢問行李的件數，baggage 或 luggage 表示「要托運的行李」，而 hand baggage 或 carry-on 表示「會帶上飛機的隨身行李」。

How many bags?

Track 560

你有幾件行李？

▶ I have one luggage and one hand baggage.

我有一件托運行李和一件隨身行李。

▶ Does my luggage go directly to Taipei?

我的行李會直接運到台北嗎？

May I change seats?

Track 561

我可以換座位嗎？

▶ Can I sit over there?

我可以坐那裡嗎？

▶ Can I go sit there instead?

我可以坐到那裡去嗎？

instead 表示「替代」的意思，在例句中意指坐到另一個位子替代原位。

Can I put this here?

Track 562

我可以把這個放在這裡嗎？

▶ Can I put my bag under my seat?

我可以把包包放在椅子下嗎？

▶ Will you put this somewhere for me?

可不可以幫我把這個放在某個地方？

Will you... 為另一種表達請求的方式，表示「麻煩你……」。

May I have a glass of water? *Track 563*

我可以要一杯水嗎？

▶ Apple juice, please.
　請給我蘋果汁。

▶ Is the beer free?
　啤酒是免費的嗎？

目前機上除了供應咖啡和紅茶之外，也經常會提供中式的茶，此時為了區別，空服人員會稱紅茶為 black tea 或 English tea「英國茶」；稱中式的茶為 jasmine tea「茉莉花茶」或 Chinese tea「中國茶」。

Coffee or tea? *Track 564*

請問要喝咖啡還是茶？

▶ Tea with milk, please.
　請給我紅茶加牛奶。

▶ I'll have coffee.
　我要咖啡。

What time will we arrive in Vancouver? *Track 565*

我們幾點會到溫哥華？

▶ What time is it in L.A. now?
　洛杉磯現在幾點？

▶ What's the local time now?
　當地時間現在幾點？

Do you have Chinese newspapers? *Track 566*

你們有中文報紙嗎？

▶ Do you have any magazines?
　你們有任何雜誌嗎？

▶ Do you have the catalogue of duty-free goods?
　有免稅品的目錄嗎？

Are you going to visit other countries?

Track 567

你還會去其他國家嗎？

▶ I'll visit Germany and France during this trip.
此行我還會去德國和法國。

▶ This will be the only country I visit.
我只會待在這個國家。

▶ We'll stay in this country only.
我們只會待在這個國家。

What's the value of these three cameras?

Track 568

這三台相機價值多少？

▶ What's the value of this laptop?
這台筆記型電腦價值多少？

▶ How much is this worth?
這東西值多少錢？

Can I go now?

Track 569

我可以走了嗎？

▶ May I leave now? 我可以離開了嗎？

▶ Is it ok now? 都好了嗎？

Can I exchange NT dollars?

Track 570

可以使用台幣兌換嗎？

▶ Do you accept NT dollars? 你們接受台幣嗎？

▶ Do you take US dollars? 你們接受美金嗎？

What's the exchange rate for NT dollars?

Track 571

台幣的匯率是多少？

exchange 表示「交換」，而 exchange rate 則是「匯率」的意思。

▶ What's the exchange rate? 匯率是多少？
▶ What's the rate to exchange NT dollars into Euros?
台幣換歐元的匯率是多少？

Do you charge for exchange?

Track 572

要收手續費嗎？

▶ Is there an extra fee? 要額外收費嗎？
▶ Is there an additional fee? 要加收費用嗎？

Can I cash my traveler's checks here?

Track 573

我可以在這裡兌換旅支嗎？

Is it possible... 為禮貌性詢問「可不可能」的意思。

▶ Is it possible to cash my traveler's checks here?
我能不能在這裡兌換旅行支票？
▶ Could you cash my traveler's checks?
你能將我的旅行支票兌現嗎？

Are you still open?

Track 574

你們還有營業嗎？

opening hours 或 office hours 皆表示「營業時間」的意思。

▶ When will you close? 你們幾點休息？
▶ What are your opening hours?
你們的營業時間是幾點到幾點？
▶ What are your office hours?
請問你們的營業時間？

Are you open on weekends?
Track 575

你們週末有營業嗎？
- ▶ Where can I exchange money on weekends?
  週末哪裡可以換錢？
- ▶ Is there a place where I can exchange money on weekends?
  有週末可以換錢的地方嗎？

Where can I find a baggage cart?
Track 576

哪裡有行李推車？
- ▶ Please get one trolley for me.
  請幫我推一台推車來。

> baggage cart 和 trolley 皆表示「行李推車」的意思，後者乃英式英語常見說法。

Will you carry my baggage?
Track 577

請幫我搬行李好嗎？
- ▶ Can you carry my baggage for me?
  你能幫我搬行李嗎？
- ▶ Can you help me with my two bags?
  能請你幫我拿這兩個袋子嗎？
- ▶ Can you help me, please? 能請你幫我嗎？

Where is the taxi stand?
Track 578

計程車招呼站在哪裡？
- ▶ Where can I get a bus? 哪裡可以搭公車？
- ▶ Which bus goes downtown?
  幾號公車有到市中心？
- ▶ Where is the nearest subway station?
  最近的地鐵站在哪裡？

> 「搭乘」固然可用 take，但在口語表達時多用 get。

> 捷運、地鐵的美式說法是 subway 或 metro，英式說法則是 underground 或 tube。

Do I have to get a ticket first?
Track 579

我要先買票嗎？

▶ Can I pay on the bus?
可以上車付現嗎？

get off 表示「下車、離開」的意思。

▶ Please give the ticket back when you get off.
下車時請繳回票根。

What's the best way to get there?
Track 580

怎麼去那裡最好？

▶ Is it easy to take a bus?
搭公車容易嗎？

▶ How much will it cost to take a taxi?
搭計程車要多少錢呢？

你可以這樣說

Hi! I'd like to check in.
Track 581

你好，我要辦登機手續。

check in 表示「辦理登記、報到」，常用於飯店住房登記或是機場櫃台登機報到。

▶ Can we check in here?
我們可以在這裡辦登機手續嗎？

▶ Is this the right counter to check in at?
在這個櫃台辦登機手續對嗎？

I'm transferring to Chicago.
Track 582

我要轉機到芝加哥。

▶ We're transferring to Sydney.
我們要轉機到雪梨。

▶ I'm a transfer passenger.
我是個要轉機的乘客。

Here is my ticket.
Track 583

這是我的機票。

▶ Here is my E-ticket number.
這是我的電子機票號碼。

▶ Here is my member card. 這是我的會員卡。

▶ Let me get my passport. 我找一下我的護照。

I've booked special meals.
Track 584

我有訂特別餐食。

▶ I've booked vegetarian meals.
我訂了素食餐。

▶ We ordered high fiber meals.
我們訂了高纖維餐。

Here is your boarding pass.
Track 585

這是你的登機證。

▶ Please give me my boarding pass. 請給我登機證。

▶ You forgot to give me my boarding pass.
你忘了把登機證給我。

Please go to Gate 5.
Track 586

請前往五號登機門。

▶ How do I get to Gate 5 from here?
從這裡要怎麼前往五號登機門？

▶ How long does it take to walk from here?
從這裡走過去要多久？

▶ When is my boarding time?
我什麼時候要登機？

> boarding 表示
> 「登機」的意
> 思，登機前除了
> 護照還需出示
> boarding pass
> 「登機證」。

Someone is sitting in my seat.

▣ Track 587

有人坐我的位子。

May I... 為禮貌性的請求，表示「我能不能、可不可以」。

▶ Excuse me. Are you sure you are in the right seat?
　　不好意思，你確定你坐對座位嗎？

▶ May I see your boarding pass?
　　我可以看一下你的登機證嗎？

I need a blanket.

▣ Track 588

我需要一條毛毯。

▶ I need an extra pillow.
　　我需要另一個枕頭。

▶ I don't have a headset.
　　我沒有耳機。

Please put the tray table down.

▣ Track 589

請把餐桌放下來。

▶ Would you like beef or chicken?
　　請問要吃牛肉還是雞肉？

▶ Beef for me and chicken for my wife.
　　請給我牛肉，然後給我太太雞肉。

▶ Pasta, please.
　　請給我義大利麵。

The seat belt sign is on.

▣ Track 590

扣緊安全帶的燈號亮了。

fasten 表示「扣緊、繫好」的意思。

▶ Please fasten your seat belt.
　　請扣好你的安全帶。

▶ My seat belt is fastened.
　　我的安全帶已經扣好了。

This is my first time in Canada. ◀ Track 591
這是我第一次來加拿大。
▶ This is my first visit here.
　這是我第一次來這裡。
▶ This is our first time here.
　這是我們第一次來這裡。

I'll be here for about two weeks. ◀ Track 592
我會待上兩星期。
▶ I'll stay for a month.
　我會待上一個月。
▶ We plan to stay for ten days.
　我們打算待十天。
▶ My return flight is in three days.
　我的回程飛機是在三天之後。

The purpose of my visit is sightseeing. ◀ Track 593
我此行是為了觀光。
▶ I'm here to visit friends.
　我是來拜訪朋友的。
▶ I'm here to travel.
　我是來旅行的。
▶ I'm here on business.
　我是來洽商的。
▶ I'm here to attend a wedding.
　我是來參加婚禮的。

attend 表示「參加某典禮、場合」的意思。

I'm going to stay at hotels.

◀ *Track 594*

我會住在飯店。

▶ I'll stay at youth hostels.
我會住在青年旅館。

▶ I'm going to stay with my friend. Here is her address.
我會住在朋友家，這裡是她的地址。

stay 表示「暫留、小住」的意思。

I forgot to fill in this form.

◀ *Track 595*

我忘了填這張表。

▶ I didn't have this form.
我沒有這張表格。

▶ I'll fill it in right now.
我現在馬上填寫。

This is my wife.

◀ *Track 596*

這是我太太。

▶ This is my kid.
這是我的小孩。

▶ We are together.
我們是一起的。

I came from Hong Kong.

◀ *Track 597*

我從香港飛來。

▶ My flight number is CA501.
我的班機號碼是 CA501。

▶ I can't remember my flight number. It is Eva Air from Taipei.
我不記得我的班機號碼，是從台北飛來的長榮班機。

The baggage claim area is this way. ◀ *Track 598*
行李提領區往這邊。
▶ Where is the baggage claim?
要到哪裡提領行李？
▶ How do I get to the baggage claim?
我要怎麼到行李提領區？

> claim 表示「認領、索取」的意思；baggage claim 則是機場出關前的「行李提領區」。

Our baggage claim is at 6A. ◀ *Track 599*
我們的行李轉盤是 6A。
▶ We should go to 6A for our baggage.
我們應該去 6A 領行李。
▶ Let's meet at baggage claim 6A.
我們在行李轉盤 6A 碰面。

I have nothing to declare. ◀ *Track 600*
我沒有東西需要申報。
▶ I have something to declare.
我有東西需要申報。
▶ I'm not sure if I need to declare.
我不確定我是否需要申報。

> declare 表示「申報、宣稱」的意思。

I have one bottle of whiskey. ◀ *Track 601*
我有一瓶威士忌。
▶ I have one carton of cigarettes.
我有一條香菸。
▶ We have three cartons of cigarettes altogether.
我們總共有三條香菸。

> carton 是「紙盒、紙箱」的意思，也是一條香菸的單位詞。

This is for my own use.

Track 602

這是我要自己用的。

for one's use
表示「給某人
使用」的
意思。

▶ This is for personal use.
　這是個人使用的。

▶ They are gifts for my family.
　這些是要給家人的禮物。

These are Chinese medicines.

Track 603

這些是中藥。

▶ It's medicine for sore throats.
　這是喉嚨痛的藥。

▶ That's medicine for the stomach.
　那是胃藥。

I'd like to exchange 30,000 NT dollars.

Track 604

我想換三萬元台幣。

▶ Let me think how much I should exchange.
　讓我想一下應該要換多少錢。

▶ I'm not sure if 30,000 is enough.
　我不確定換三萬元夠不夠。

Please give me all twenty dollar bills.

Track 605

請都給我二十元的紙鈔。

▶ Please give me one fifty and five tens.
　請給我一張五十和五張十元的紙鈔。

bill 表示「鈔
票」或「帳單」
的意思。

▶ I'd like smaller bills.
　請給我小鈔。

I didn't know there is a shuttle bus. ◀ *Track 606*

我不知道有機場巴士。

▶ We should take the shuttle bus.
我們應該搭機場巴士。

▶ We can take the shuttle bus next time.
下一次可以搭機場巴士。

> shuttle bus 為定點接送服務的巴士，包括機場巴士或其他種類的接駁車。

Our hotel should have a pickup service. ◀ *Track 607*

飯店應該有接機服務啊。

▶ I saw the mini bus from our hotel.
我看到我們飯店派來的小巴士了。

▶ Are you here to pick us up?
請問你是來接我們的嗎？

> pick up 表示「拾起、接人」的意思。

你可以這樣問

Excuse me! Where is the bus stop? ◀ *Track 608*

請問一下！公車站在哪裡？

▶ How can I get to the bus stop?
　公車站怎麼走？

▶ Where can I find the nearest bus stop?
　最近的公車站在哪裡？

▶ I won't go out on my own.　我不會自己一個人出去。

Do I have to buy a ticket before getting on the bus? ◀ *Track 609*

要在上車前先買票嗎？

▶ Can I pay on the bus?　我可以上車再付嗎？

▶ I don't have any change.　我沒有零錢。

change 除了常見表示「改變」的意思，在這裡是當名詞，表示「零錢」的意思。

Do I need to validate this ticket? ◀ *Track 610*

需要先讓車票生效嗎？

▶ Is there a machine for validating?
　有生效用的機器嗎？

▶ Do I not need to validate the ticket?
　不必有車票生效手續嗎？

validate 表示「使生效、確認」的意思。

Do I need the exact change? ◀ *Track 611*

需要有剛好的零錢嗎？

▶ Do you need the exact amount?
　你只收正確的金額嗎？

▶ Here is the exact change.　這裡的零錢剛好。

Is it cheaper to buy a day pass?
🔊 *Track 612*

買一日票有沒有比較便宜？

▶ Should I get a day pass?
我該不該買一日票？

▶ May I get a day pass?
請給我一張一日票好嗎？

Can you tell me where to get off?
🔊 *Track 613*

請告訴我在哪裡下車好嗎？

▶ Please tell me where to get off.
請告訴我在哪裡下車。

▶ Please tell me when we are at the train station.
到火車站時請告訴我。

> get off 表示
> 「下車、下班」
> 的意思。

Do I need to change lines?
🔊 *Track 614*

需要換線嗎？

▶ Do I need to change trains?
要換火車嗎？

▶ Do I need to change buses?
要換公車嗎？

> line 除了「線、
> 行列」的意思，
> 在此是表示「路
> 線」的意思。

How long will it take?
🔊 *Track 615*

多久會到？

▶ How long is the journey? 旅程要多久呢？

▶ When will we arrive? 什麼時候會到？

▶ What time will we get there? 我們什麼時候會到？

Which station should I change at? ◀ *Track 616*

要在哪一站換車？

▶ Where can I change to the blue line?
　我可以在哪裡換藍線？

▶ Where should I get off?
　我要在哪裡下車？

▶ Should I change at the next station?
　我應該在下一站換車嗎？

When is the last bus? ◀ *Track 617*

末班公車是幾點？

▶ When is the last train? 最後一班火車是幾點？

▶ When is the latest I can return?
　回程最晚幾點？

Where is the ticket office? ◀ *Track 618*

售票口在哪裡？

▶ Where can I get tickets? 哪裡可以買票？

▶ Where can I get tickets for today?
　哪裡可以買今日的票？

▶ Where can I get tickets for next week?
　哪裡可以買下禮拜的票？

Can I buy a ticket for tomorrow? ◀ *Track 619*

我可以買明天的票嗎？

▶ Two tickets for tomorrow, please.
　請給我兩張明天的票。

▶ Can I get a ticket for next Monday?
　可以買下禮拜一的票嗎？

Can I get a second class ticket?
🔊 *Track 620*

可以買一張二等艙的票嗎？

▶ Can I get a first class ticket?
可以買一張頭等艙的票嗎？

▶ Are there still seats for the second class?
二等艙還有位子嗎？

▶ Are there any seats available? 還有位子嗎？

> available 表示「有空的、在手邊」的意思。

Do I have to reserve a seat?
🔊 *Track 621*

需要先劃位嗎？

▶ Do we need to reserve seats? 我們需要先劃位嗎？

▶ I'd like to reserve a seat. 我要劃位。

What platform does it leave from?
🔊 *Track 622*

從哪一個月台出發？

▶ Where is my platform?
我的月台在哪裡？

▶ Which platform should I go to?
我要到哪一個月台？

▶ Does the train to New York leave from Platform 5?
去紐約的火車在五號月台嗎？

> platform 表示火車、電車、地鐵的乘客上下車的「月台」。

How many stops are there?
🔊 *Track 623*

總共有幾站？

▶ How many stops in total? 全部一共有幾站？

▶ How many stops are there on this line?
這條線有幾站啊？

> in total 表示「全部加起來、總共」的意思。

How many ferries leave every day? ◀ *Track 624*

每天有幾班渡輪？

▶ **How often do they leave?**
出發間隔多久？

▶ **When is the next ferry?**
下一班渡輪是幾點？

How long till the next departure? ◀ *Track 625*

還要多久有下一班？

▶ **Do I have to wait long for the next one?**
要等很久才有下一班嗎？

▶ **When is the next one?**
下一班是幾點？

departure
表示「出發、離開」的意思，也可以當作「下一班離開的公車、火車、渡輪或飛機」。

How much is it to take the car? ◀ *Track 626*

車子上渡輪要多少錢？

▶ **How much do you charge for the car?**
帶車子要收多少錢嗎？

▶ **How many cars do you take?**
可以載幾部車子？

Is there a restaurant on board? ◀ *Track 627*

渡輪上有餐廳嗎？

▶ **Can I get some food on the ferry?**
渡輪上有賣東西吃嗎？

▶ **Where can I find the restaurant?**
餐廳在哪裡？

▶ **Do you have anything hot?**
有熱食嗎？

on board 表示「在船、火車、飛機上」的意思。

When do I have to arrive?
🔊 *Track 628*

幾點要到？

▶ How early should I arrive?
我多早要到？

▶ What time should I get here?
我幾點要到？

▶ When is the boarding time?
幾點可以開始上船？

Where do I check in?
🔊 *Track 629*

要到哪裡辦登機手續？

▶ Where is the check-in counter?
辦理登機櫃台在哪裡？

▶ Where to check in? 在哪裡辦登機手續？

How many bags can I take?
🔊 *Track 630*

可以帶幾件行李？

▶ How many bags are allowed?
能帶幾件行李呢？

▶ Are three bags ok? 帶三個袋子可以嗎？

▶ What should I do with the extra bag?
多帶的這個袋子怎麼辦？

Is it cheaper to fly on a Sunday?
🔊 *Track 631*

禮拜天的機票比較便宜嗎？

▶ When is it cheaper to fly? 哪個時段的機票比較便宜？

▶ Can you check for a cheaper flight?
可以幫我查便宜一點的班機嗎？

Can I change it to a later flight?
▶ *Track 632*

可以改晚一點的班機嗎？

▶ Can I catch a later flight?
可以搭晚一點的班機嗎？

▶ Can I change it to the next flight?
可以改成下一班嗎？

What's the expected arrival time?
▶ *Track 633*

預計抵達時間是幾點？

▶ What time does it land?
幾點會降落？

▶ When do we get there?
幾點到啊？

> land 一般是當名詞，表示「土地」的意思，在此是當作動詞，表示「降落」的意思。

Can I get an upgrade?
▶ *Track 634*

我可以升等嗎？

▶ Is there a seat with more leg room?
有沒有寬一點的位子？

▶ Is this flight full?
這班飛機有客滿嗎？

> with more leg room 就是表示「座位有較大讓雙腿伸展的空間」。

Are drinks included?
▶ *Track 635*

機票有包含飲料嗎？

▶ Are drinks free?
飲料是免費的嗎？

▶ Is the liquor free?
酒是免費的嗎？

> liquor 表示「酒、含酒精的飲料」的意思。

Can you help me get my bag down? ◀ *Track 636*
可以幫我把袋子拿下來嗎？

▶ Can you reach my bag?
你拿得到我的袋子嗎？

▶ Can you see a red backpack in there?
你有沒有看到裡面有個紅色的背包？

Where can I find a taxi? ◀ *Track 637*
哪裡叫得到計程車？

▶ Where can I get a cab? 哪裡搭得到計程車？

How much does it cost to go to the ◀ *Track 638* British Museum?
到大英博物館多少錢？

▶ How much is it to the train station?
到火車站多少錢？

▶ How much is it to the airport? 到機場多少錢？

Can I order a taxi, please? ◀ *Track 639*
麻煩您，我要叫車。

▶ When will it arrive? 幾點會到？

▶ There are three of us. 我們有三個人。

Can you take me to the airport? ◀ *Track 640*
麻煩到機場好嗎？

▶ Can you take me to the bus terminal?
麻煩到客運總站好嗎？

Can you wait outside?

Track 641

能麻煩你在外面等嗎？

▶ Can you wait, please?
能麻煩你等一下嗎？

▶ It won't take long.　不會太久。

shortcut 表示
「捷徑、近路」
的意思。

Is there a quicker way?

Track 642

有沒有快一點的路線？

▶ Is there a shortcut?
有沒有捷徑？

in a hurry 表示
「趕時間、匆
忙」的意思。

▶ I'm in a hurry.
我在趕時間。

Can you drop me off here?

Track 643

可以讓我在這裡下車嗎？

drop off 表示
「讓……下
車」的意思。

▶ Can I get off here?
我可以在這裡下車嗎？

▶ Please stop here.
請在這裡停車。

Can you pick me up again tomorrow?

Track 644

可以請你明天再來載我嗎？

▶ Can you collect me again tomorrow?
明天可以再來載我嗎？

pick up 表示
「載人、撿起」
的意思。

▶ Can I order your service again for tomorrow?
我明天可以再麻煩你嗎？

Where can I rent a car?

Track 645

哪裡可以租車？

▶ Where can I find a car rental?
哪裡有租車行？

▶ I saw couple car rentals outside the airport.
我在機場外面看到好幾家租車行。

car rental 表示「租車行、租車的地方」的意思。

Am I insured?

Track 646

我有保險嗎？

▶ Am I included in the insurance?
保險有保到我嗎？

▶ What's covered by the insurance?
保險的範圍包括哪些？

Can my wife drive as well?

Track 647

我太太也可以開嗎？

▶ Can we both drive?
我們兩個人都可以開嗎？

▶ Can he drive too?
他也可以開嗎？

Do I need to fill the tank before returning it?

Track 648

還車前油要加滿嗎？

▶ Is the tank full? 油箱是滿的嗎？

▶ Do I need to fill the tank first?
要先加油嗎？

▶ Is the tank empty? 油箱有油嗎？

tank 表示「油箱、油槽」的意思。

What kind of fuel does it take?
Track 649

要加哪一種油？
- ▶ Is it a diesel car?
  這是柴油車嗎？
- ▶ It only takes unleaded gasoline.
  只能加無鉛汽油。

汽車的燃料分為許多種，包括：diesel「柴油」，unleaded gasoline「無鉛汽油」等。

Do you have an automatic?
Track 650

有自排車嗎？
- ▶ I prefer automatic.
  我喜歡自排車。
- ▶ I'll take a manual shift one.
  我要租手排車。

automatic 自動的，表示「自排車」的意思；manual shift 手動換檔，表示「手排車」的意思。

你可以這樣說

My headphones don't work.
Track 651

我的耳機壞了。
- ▶ Can I get a new pair?　請給我一副新的好嗎？
- ▶ Please get me a new pair.
  請幫我拿一副新的。

pair 表示「一副、一對、一雙」的意思，因耳機有左右兩耳，故單位詞為 pair。

Here is my driver's license.
Track 652

這是我的駕照。
- ▶ Here is a copy of my driver's license.
  這是我的駕照印本。
- ▶ I don't have my driver's license with me now.
  我現在身上沒帶駕照。

driver's license 或 driving license 都是「駕照」的意思。

I'd like to rent a car.

◀ *Track 653*

我想租一台車。

▶ We'd like to rent a car for three days.
我們想要租車租三天。

▶ We'd like to rent this car for a week.
這台車我們想要租一個禮拜。

NOTE

你可以這樣問

Do you have a double room free? ◀ *Track 654*

還有雙人房嗎？

▶ Can I have a room for two?
可以訂一間雙人房嗎？

double room
指的是有一張
雙人床的「雙
人房」。

▶ I need a room for two.
我需要一間雙人房。

▶ Do you have a room for both of us?
有可以讓我們兩個人住的房間嗎？

• •

Do you have a twin room? ◀ *Track 655*

有兩人房嗎？

▶ We need two separate beds.
我們需要兩張床。

twin room 指
的是有兩張單
人床的「兩人
房」。

▶ Can we add an extra bed?
可以再加一張床嗎？

▶ Do you charge for an extra bed?
加床要加價嗎？

• •

Could you show me the room? ◀ *Track 656*

可以帶我們看一下房間嗎？

▶ Can I take a look?
我可以看一下嗎？

look around
表示「四處看
看」的意思。

▶ May I see the room first?
我可以先看房間嗎？

▶ Could I have a look around?
我可以先四處看看嗎？

• •

How much does it cost for one night?

🔊 *Track 657*

住一個晚上要多少錢？

▶ What's the price per night?
每晚房價多少？

▶ How much for a room?
每房多少錢？

▶ How much for a one night stay?
住一晚多少錢？

Do you have parking?

🔊 *Track 658*

有停車位嗎？

▶ Can I park my car nearby?
我車子可以停在附近嗎？

▶ Is there a place to park near the hotel?
旅館附近有停車的地方嗎？

▶ Where can I park?
哪裡可以停車？

Is breakfast included?

🔊 *Track 659*

有包含早餐嗎？

▶ Do you provide breakfast?
有提供早餐嗎？

▶ How much is breakfast?
早餐多少錢？

▶ I'd like to order breakfast too.
我也要預訂早餐。

May I bring my pet?

🔊 *Track 660*

可以帶寵物嗎？

accommodate 表示「容納、提供食宿」的意思。

▶ **Are dogs allowed?** 可以帶狗嗎？

▶ **Can you accommodate pets?**
你有提供寵物住宿嗎？

▶ **What are your rules about pets?**
關於寵物有什麼規則？

Is the room en suite?

🔊 *Track 661*

是套房嗎？

▶ **Does the room have a shower?**
房間內有浴室嗎？

▶ **Does the room have a bath?** 房間裡有浴缸嗎？

Can I get help with my bags?

🔊 *Track 662*

有人能幫我提行李嗎？

porter 表示「提行李服務員、挑夫」的意思。

▶ **Do you have a porter?** 有提行李服務員嗎？

▶ **My bags are in the car.** 我的行李在車子裡。

▶ **I need help with my luggage.**
我需要有人幫我拿行李。

Can we stay an extra night?

🔊 *Track 663*

我們可以再住一天嗎？

▶ **I'd like to change the number of nights.**
我要更改天數。

extend 表示「延長」的意思。

▶ **May I extend my stay?** 可以延長住房嗎？

▶ **I want to leave on Wednesday.** 我要到禮拜三離開。

What time is check out?

Track 664

幾點要退房？

▶ When do we have to be out of the room?
幾點要離開房間？

▶ When do we have to leave?　幾點必須離開？

▶ When do we have the room till?
可以到幾點退房？

Which floor is it on?

Track 665

房間在幾樓？

▶ How do I find the room?　房間在哪裡？

▶ Do you have a map of the hotel?
有旅館的位置圖嗎？

▶ Can you show me the way?　請告訴我在哪裡？

> show someone the way 表示「為某人指路」的意思。

Do you have an extra key?

Track 666

有多的鑰匙嗎？

▶ Can we have two keys?　我們可以有兩支鑰匙嗎？

▶ Can we both have a key?　我們可以一人有一支鑰匙嗎？

Do you have a safe?

Track 667

有保險箱嗎？

▶ Is there somewhere to store valuables?
有放貴重物品的地方嗎？

▶ Can I leave this with you?
這可以請你保管嗎？

▶ Do you have secure lockers?
你們有安全的寄物櫃嗎？

> valuable 表示「值錢、貴重物品」的意思。

Where is the restaurant?

Track 668

餐廳在哪裡？

▶ Where do we eat?
在哪裡用餐？

▶ Where is breakfast served?
早餐在哪裡吃？

▶ Which way to the restaurant?
餐廳從哪裡走？

Is there a laundry service?

Track 669

laundry 表示「洗衣房、待洗衣物」的意思。

有送洗服務嗎？

▶ I have some clothes I need washing.
我有衣服需要洗。

▶ Do you have laundry facilities?
有洗衣設備嗎？

facility 表示「設備、設施」的意思。

▶ Can I get some clothes washed?
我能洗衣服嗎？

Is there a gym?

Track 670

有健身房嗎？

▶ Do you have a gym?
這裡有健身房嗎？

▶ Do I need to bring my own towel?
我需要自己帶毛巾嗎？

sauna 是「三溫暖」的意思。

▶ Is there a sauna inside?
裡面有三溫暖嗎？

Is the reception 24 hours?

Track 671

櫃台是二十四小時嗎？

▶ What time do we need to be back at night?
我們晚上需要在幾點前回來？

▶ Can we come and go at any time?
可以自由進出嗎？

▶ Can I get back in after eleven?
十一點之後還進的來嗎？

Is there a bar?
🔊 *Track 672*

有酒吧嗎？

▶ Do you serve drinks?
有賣飲料嗎？

▶ What time does the bar close?
酒吧幾點休息？

Can I get a massage?
🔊 *Track 673*

可以預約按摩嗎？

▶ Can I order a massage session?
可以預約一個按摩療程嗎？

▶ May I book a spa session?
可以預約 spa 嗎？

▶ Can I have the massage in my room?
按摩可以在房間內進行嗎？

Do you have a day-care center?
🔊 *Track 674*

有托兒中心嗎？

▶ Can I leave my kids with you?
我可以把小孩托給你們嗎？

▶ Do you have babysitting service?
有托兒服務嗎？

Can I order room service?

🔊 *Track 675*

我可以叫客房服務嗎?

room service
表示飯店內的
各式「客房服
務」。

▶ I'd like room service. 我需要客房服務。

▶ What's the number for room service?
客房服務的電話號碼是幾號?

▶ Room service, please. 請給我客房服務。

Can I get breakfast in my room?

🔊 *Track 676*

我可以在房間用早餐嗎?

▶ Breakfast for Room 27, please.
請送早餐到 27 號房。

▶ I'd like to order breakfast in my room.
我想在房間裡點早餐。

▶ Can I get a late breakfast?
可以晚一點送早餐嗎?

What time do you serve till?

🔊 *Track 677*

服務時間到幾點?

available 表
示「可得到、
在手邊」的意
思。

▶ What time is room service available?
客房服務的時間是幾點到幾點?

▶ Are you still serving food? 還有供應餐點嗎?

Can I get my room cleaned?

🔊 *Track 678*

可以來打掃房間嗎?

maid 表示「女
侍、女傭」的
意思。

▶ My bed has not been made. 我的床鋪沒有整理。

▶ The maid has not been to my room.
客房打掃人員還沒來過。

▶ The room needs cleaning. 房間需要打掃。

Can I order a morning newspaper? ◀ *Track 679*

我可以訂一份早報嗎？

▶ Do you supply newspapers?
有供應報紙嗎？

▶ Please deliver my newspaper to Room 601.
請把報紙送到 601 號房。

▶ Can you put it under my door?
可以從門下塞進來嗎？

> under the door 就表示「在門下面」的意思。

Do you have lost property? ◀ *Track 680*

有失物招領嗎？

▶ I've lost my glasses.
我的眼鏡掉了。

▶ I've left my cell phone behind at the bar.
我把手機忘在酒吧裡。

▶ Have you seen my camera?
有看到我的相機嗎？

> leave behind 表示「忘了帶、留下」的意思。

Can we check out later? ◀ *Track 681*

我們可以晚一點退房嗎？

▶ Can we keep the room for two more hours?
房間可以多保留兩小時嗎？

▶ Can we stay for a bit longer?
可以待晚一點嗎？

▶ Is it alright to check out later?
晚一點退房可以嗎？

> check out 表示「退房、結帳離開」的意思。

Can I pay by credit card?

🔊 *Track 682*

可以用信用卡嗎？

▶ Here is my card.
這是我的信用卡。

▶ Do you accept cards?
你們收信用卡嗎？

▶ May I use Mastercard?
可以用萬事達卡嗎？

Can I have a receipt?

🔊 *Track 683*

可以給我收據嗎？

▶ Can I get a copy of the bill?
可以給我一份帳單的副本嗎？

▶ I need an itemized receipt.
我需要一張收據細目。

> itemize 表示
> 「分條、詳細
> 列舉」的
> 意思。

May we leave our bags?

🔊 *Track 684*

可以把袋子寄在這裡嗎？

▶ Can we collect these later?
這些可以晚一點再過來拿嗎？

▶ Where can we leave our luggage?
哪裡可以寄放行李？

> collect 在此表
> 示「領取」的
> 意思。

Do you have a guestbook?

🔊 *Track 685*

有訪客留言本嗎？

▶ Can I write in the guestbook?
我可以寫訪客留言本嗎？

▶ I want to write a note in your guestbook.
我想要在訪客留言本裡留言。

> guestbook 是
> 一些民宿、青
> 年旅館會提供
> 來訪房客留言
> 的「訪客留言
> 本」。

▶ I've written in the guestbook.
我已經寫了訪客留言本。

Do you have shuttle service to the airport?

◀ *Track 686*

有接駁車到機場嗎？

▶ What time is the next shuttle bus?
下一班接駁車是幾點？

▶ How do I get to the train station?
要怎麼去火車站？

Can you book a cab for me?

◀ *Track 687*

可以幫我預約計程車嗎？

▶ Can you call a taxi for me?
可以幫我叫計程車嗎？

▶ Where can I get a taxi?
哪裡可以叫到計程車？

你可以這樣說

I'd like to make a reservation.

◀ *Track 688*

我要訂房。

▶ Can I book a room?
我要訂一個房間。

▶ Do you have any rooms free?
還有房間嗎？

▶ Do you have any vacancies?
還有空房嗎？

vacancy 表示「空
房、缺額」。

I made a booking.
Track 689

我有訂房。

▶ We have a reservation. 我們有訂房。

▶ I booked under the name Michael Brown.
我是用麥克布朗的名字訂房。

▶ I called earlier to book a room.
我之前有打電話來訂房。

under the name 表示「用什麼名字」的意思。

My name is Lily Fan.
Track 690

我的名字是范莉莉。

▶ I booked a room under the name Lily Fan.
我用范莉莉的名字訂了一間房。

▶ You should have a room for Mr. Huang.
你應該會看到黃先生訂的房。

Here are my passport details.
Track 691

這是我的護照資料。

▶ Do you need to see my ID? 需要看身份證件嗎？

▶ Shall I fill this in? 需要填這個嗎？

▶ Where do I sign? 要在哪裡簽名？

fill in 表示「填寫表格」的意思。

I'd like a new towel.
Track 692

我需要一條新的毛巾。

▶ Can we get clean towels? 可以給我們新的毛巾嗎？

▶ Our towels need replacing.
我們的毛巾需要換了。

▶ Can you bring up a clean towel?
可以送一條乾淨的毛巾上來嗎？

I need an extra pillow.

Track 693

我還需要一個枕頭。

▶ Can I get an extra pillow?
可以多給我一個枕頭嗎？

▶ I don't have enough pillows. 我的枕頭不夠。

▶ May I have an extra pillow brought up?
可以幫我多送一個枕頭上來嗎？

I'd like to make a complaint.

Track 694

我要客訴。

▶ Can I talk to the manager? 我可以找經理談嗎？

▶ I'm not happy with my room. 我對我的房間不滿意。

▶ This is not what I expected. 這不是我所期望的。

complaint 表示
「客訴、抱怨、
抗議」的意思。

There is no hot water.

Track 695

根本沒有熱水。

▶ I can't get any hot water. 完全沒有熱水。

▶ The water is not hot at all. 水一點都不熱。

▶ The hot water isn't working. 熱水沒有用。

at all 表示「一點
也不」的意思。

The air conditioning is not working.

Track 696

空調壞掉了。

▶ The room is too hot. 房間好熱喔。

▶ The room is too cold. 房間好冷喔。

▶ Can you fix the heating? 可以來修暖氣嗎？

▶ Can you send someone to fix it?
可以派人來修一下嗎？

air conditioning
表示「空調設備」
的意思。

I can't get on the Internet.

沒辦法上網。

Track 697

▶ How do I log on to the Internet?
要怎麼登入網路？

▶ The Internet connection isn't working.
網路連不上。

▶ My Internet code failed.
網路代碼無法使用。

My room is too noisy.

我的房間很吵。

Track 698

▶ I can't sleep because of the noise.
太吵了我沒辦法睡覺。

▶ Is there a quieter room?
有沒有比較安靜的房間？

▶ There is a lot of noise in my room.
我的房間有很多雜音。

I'm not feeling well.

我不太舒服。

Track 699

▶ Can you call a doctor?
可以幫我請醫生來嗎？

▶ I think I need a doctor.
我想我需要請醫生。

▶ Can we get some medical help?
我們可以請求醫療協助嗎？

I didn't use this.

我沒有用這個啊。

Track 700

▶ **This shouldn't be on my bill.**
帳單上不應該有這個啊。

▶ **Can you explain this charge?**
可以解釋一下這筆收費嗎？

▶ **What is this cost for?**
這是什麼費用？

▶ **I didn't make this phone call.**
我沒有打這通電話。

I forgot my passport in the safe.   ◀ *Track 701*
我把護照忘在保險箱裡。

▶ **Can I have my passport back?**
可以幫我去拿護照嗎？

▶ **Can I have my things from the safe?**
可以幫我把東西從保險箱取出來嗎？

> safe 除了「安全的、沒有危險的」，在此當作名詞，表示「保險箱」的意思。

There is no toilet paper in the toilet.◀ *Track 702*
廁所沒有衛生紙了。

▶ **The toilet is blocked.** 馬桶堵塞了。

▶ **The toilet needs cleaning.**
廁所需要清潔。

Please keep the change.   ◀ *Track 703*
剩下的當作小費。

▶ **Keep the tip.**
小費請留著。

Chapter 05 生活體驗

你可以這樣問

Where is the post office?

◀ Track 704

郵局在哪裡？

nearby 表示「在附近」的意思。

▶ Where is the closest post office?
最近的郵局在哪裡？

▶ Is there a post office nearby? 附近有郵局嗎？

. . . .

Is the post office still open?

◀ Track 705

郵局還有開嗎？

▶ Is the bank still open? 銀行還有開嗎？

▶ When will the post office be closed? 郵局幾點關門？

. . . .

How much is this letter by air mail?

◀ Track 706

這封信寄航空多少錢？

郵寄信件、包裹有幾種不同的選擇，依送達的方式可分為：by air mail「寄航空」、by ship「寄海運」或 bysurface mail「寄水陸」等。

▶ How much is this package by air mail?
這個包裹寄航空多少錢？

▶ How much is this package by ship?
這個包裹寄海運多少錢？

▶ How much is this package by surface mail?
這個包裹寄水陸多少錢？

. . . .

Can I withdraw money with my ATM card?

◀ Track 707

我可以用金融卡提款嗎？

▶ Can I get cash with my credit card?
我可以用信用卡預借現金嗎？

▶ Can I cash my traveler's checks here?
這裡可以兌現旅行支票嗎？

. . . .

Can I make an overseas call with this telephone?

◀ *Track 708*

這台電話能打國際嗎？

▶ Can I make an international call with this phone?
這台電話能打國際電話嗎？

▶ Can I call Taiwan with this phone?
這台電話能打到台灣嗎？

How can I make a call to Taiwan?

◀ *Track 709*

打到台灣要怎麼撥？

▶ Will you tell me what to dial to make a call to Taiwan?
可以告訴我打到台灣要撥幾號嗎？

dial 表示「撥號」
的意思。

▶ Please tell me what to dial to make a call to Taipei, Taiwan.
請告訴我打到台灣台北要撥幾號。

Where can I get a phone card?

◀ *Track 710*

哪裡買得到電話卡？

▶ Do you sell phone cards?
請問有賣電話卡嗎？

▶ Do you sell phone cards for making international calls?
請問有賣打國際的電話卡嗎？

▶ Are these phone cards any different from each other?
這些電話卡有什麼不同嗎？

Can I call with my credit card?
🔊 *Track 711*

可以用信用卡打電話嗎？

▶ Can I make a credit card call?
可以打一通信用卡付費的電話嗎？

▶ I'd like to call with my credit card.
我想用信用卡打電話。

How much are the pears?
🔊 *Track 712*

梨子怎麼賣？

▶ How much is this? 這個多少錢？

▶ How much for these three? 這三樣多少錢？

▶ How much altogether? 全部多少錢？

Where can I find toothpaste?
🔊 *Track 713*

請問牙膏放在哪裡？

▶ I can't find toothpaste. 我找不到牙膏。

▶ I don't know where to find shampoo.
我找不到洗髮精。

▶ I need to get some tampons.
我要買些衛生棉條。

Where is the meeting point?
🔊 *Track 714*

我要到哪裡集合？

meeting point 表示「碰面、集合的地點」。

▶ Where is the pick-up point?
遊覽車搭乘地點在哪裡？

▶ Where should I wait for the tour bus?
我要到哪裡等遊覽車？

▶ When will they pick me up? 幾點會來載我？

Do I have to pay for re-entry? ◀╡ *Track 715*
再進場要付費嗎?

▶ Can I come back in? 我可以再入場嗎?

▶ Can I come back within the same day?
   我同一天還可以再入場嗎?

Will you take my picture? ◀╡ *Track 716*
請幫我拍張照好嗎?

▶ Will you take a picture of us?
   請幫我們拍張照嗎?

▶ Will you take a picture of me and my mom?
   請幫我和我媽媽照一張好嗎?

Can I take pictures here? ◀╡ *Track 717*
這裡可以照相嗎?

▶ Is it ok to take pictures here?
   這邊可以照相嗎?

▶ Am I allowed to take photos?
   這裡准許照相嗎?

▶ May I take photos here?
   我可以在這裡照相嗎?

Can I use flash here? ◀╡ *Track 718*
這裡可以用閃光燈嗎?

▶ Is it ok to use flash? 可以用閃光燈嗎?

▶ Am I allowed to use flash here?
   這裡准許用閃光燈嗎?

▶ May I use flash here? 我可以在這裡用閃光燈嗎?

Where are you from?

Track 719

你是哪裡人？

▶ Where do you come from? 你從哪裡來的？

▶ Where is our tour guide from?
我們的導遊是哪裡人？

▶ Where do you think she is from?
你覺得她是哪裡人？

Can I get tickets at the box office?

Track 720

現場有售票嗎？

▶ Do you sell advance tickets?
你們有賣預售票嗎？

▶ Can I get two advance tickets?
我能買兩張預售票嗎？

> advance 表示「預先的」的意思。

Can I return this ticket?

Track 721

我可以退票嗎？

▶ I'd like to return the tickets. 我想要退票。

▶ Can I change my tickets to other dates?
我的票可以改期嗎？

Is this musical still on?

Track 722

這部歌舞劇還在演嗎？

▶ Is the musical "Cats" still playing?
歌舞劇「貓」還在演嗎？

▶ Until when is this musical playing?
這部歌舞劇會演到什麼時候？

> musical 是唱作俱佳的「歌舞劇」。

How long is the performance?

🔊 *Track 723*

表演全長多長？

▶ What time will it start? 什麼時候開始？
▶ What time will it finish? 什麼時候結束？

Is there a break?

🔊 *Track 724*

有中場休息嗎？

▶ Is there an interval?
中間有休息時間嗎？
▶ How long is the interval?
中場休息時間有多久？

> break 和 interval 皆表示「中場」或「休息時間」，唯前者為美式用法，後者為英式用法。

Where can I see a stage play?

🔊 *Track 725*

哪裡可以看舞台劇？

▶ Are there any stage play theaters?
有舞台劇劇場嗎？
▶ Where can I find a stage play theater?
哪裡有舞台劇劇場？

Do you have information on current entertainment?

🔊 *Track 726*

有目前的娛樂相關資訊嗎？

▶ Do you have a brochure of current performances?
你們有目前各種表演的藝文手冊嗎？
▶ Can you tell me about this performance?
你可以介紹一下這個表演嗎？

> brochure 是介紹性的「小冊子」。

Are tickets sold at the box office? ◀€ *Track 727*

現場售票處還有在賣票嗎？

▶ Is it possible to get tickets at the box office?
現場售票處有可能買的到票嗎？

▶ Can I get tickets at the box office?
我在現場售票處買的到票嗎？

....

Is there a cover charge? ◀€ *Track 728*

cover charge
指的是「夜店
入場時收取的
費用」。

要收入場費嗎？

▶ How much is the admission?
入場費多少錢？

▶ How much is it to go in? 進去要花多少錢？

....

What do you think of Paris by night? ◀€ *Track 729*

nightscape 就
是我們常說
「萬家燈火、
霓紅閃爍的夜
景」，而另一
種常見的說法
nightlife 則表
示「夜生活的
樣貌」。

你覺得巴黎的夜如何？

▶ Where is the best place to see the nightscape of Hong Kong?
哪裡是香港看夜景最棒的地方？

▶ Where is the best place to see Hong Kong at night?
香港的夜景應該去哪裡看？

▶ Where should I go for the nightscape?
要去哪裡看夜景呢？

....

你可以這樣說

I'd like to send this postcard to Taiwan. ◀€ *Track 730*

我要寄這張明信片到台灣。

▶ How much is it to send a postcard to Taiwan?
寄一張明信片到台灣要多少錢？
▶ How much is the domestic postage?
寄國內郵資多少錢？
▶ How much is the international postage?
寄國際郵資多少錢？

postage 表示
「郵資、郵費」
的意思。

This letter is to go by express mail. ◀ *Track 731*
這封信要寄限時專送。
▶ This is an express mail.
這是限時專送。
▶ This package is to go by express mail.
這個包裹要寄快捷。

I forgot my password. ◀ *Track 732*
我忘記密碼了。
▶ I didn't know I need a password.
我不知道我需要密碼。
▶ Can I call my bank at home?
我可以打電話回國內的銀行嗎？

I want to make a call to Taiwan. ◀ *Track 733*
我想打電話回台灣。
▶ I want to call home.
我想打電話回家。
▶ I want to call my husband.
我想打電話給我先生。

make a call to 加
上國家表示「撥
打電話到某國」
的意思。

I'd like to make a collect call.

Track 734

我想打對方付費的電話。

collect call 是對方（接聽者）付費的電話。

▶ I'd like to make a collect call to Taiwan.
我想打一通對方付費的電話到台灣。

▶ I need to make a collect call.
我必須撥打對方付費的電話。

▶ Can I make a collect call here?
這裡可以打對方付費的電話嗎？

There is a telephone booth.

Track 735

那裡有電話亭。

出門在外欲撥打電話時，可尋找 telephone booth「電話亭」或是 public telephone「公共電話」。

▶ Where is the closest public telephone?
最近的公共電話在哪裡？

▶ Where can I find a public telephone?
哪裡找的到公共電話？

Let's go to the flea market.

Track 736

我們去跳蚤市場看看。

flea market 和 second-hand market 都是指賣舊貨的「二手市場」。

▶ Let's go to the second-hand market.
我們去二手市場逛逛。

▶ Second-hand markets are full of surprises.
二手市場充滿了驚喜。

▶ We can usually find surprises at second-hand markets.
二手市場經常找得到驚喜。

This is buy one get one free now.

Track 737

這個現在買一送一。

▶ This is two for one now.
這個現在買一送一。
▶ That's three for two now.
那個在買二送一。

two for one 意
指買兩個算一個
的價錢，也就是
我們的「買一送
一」，其他特惠
依此類推。

I'd like to take a one day tour to Windsor Castle.

🔊 *Track 738*

我想參加溫莎古堡一日遊。
▶ Is there a day tour to Oxford?
有去牛津的一日遊嗎？
▶ Is it a half-day or full-day tour?
這是半日遊還是一日遊？
▶ How long is this full-day tour?
這個半日遊時間多長？

Two tickets, please.

🔊 *Track 739*

請給我兩張票。
▶ Two adult tickets and one child's ticket.
兩張全票，一張兒童票。
▶ One student ticket, please. 請給我一張學生票。
▶ Do you have group tickets? 你們有團體票嗎？

I'd like to join a guided tour.

🔊 *Track 740*

我要參加導覽。
▶ I want to sign up for a guided tour.
我要登記參加導覽。
▶ We'd like to book for a guided tour.
我們想預約參加導覽。

sign up 表示「登
記參加」的意思。

audio guide 為
各大博物館、
美術館預先錄
製的「語音導
覽機」，能協
助大眾了解
展品。

I'd like to rent an audio guide.

🔊 *Track 741*

我要租借語音導覽。

▶ Renting an audio guide sounds good!
租語音導覽聽起來不錯！

▶ I have a guide book to this museum.
我有這間博物館的導覽書。

Do you mind...
表禮貌性的請
求，詢問對方
「介不介意」
的意思。

Please join me for the picture.

🔊 *Track 742*

請和我一起合照。

▶ Would you like to have your picture taken with us?
你願不願意和我們一起合照？

▶ Do you mind having a picture taken with me?
你介不介意和我一起照一張？

I'll take one more.

🔊 *Track 743*

我再照一張。

▶ I'll take a couple more so you can choose later.
我再多照幾張，然後你可以選。

▶ I'll take one more with the flash.
我用閃光燈再照一張。

We are from Taiwan.

🔊 *Track 744*

我們是台灣來的。

▶ I come from Taiwan.
我來自台灣。

▶ I'm Taiwanese.
我是台灣人。

I want to go to Bon Jovi's concert. ◀ *Track 745*

我想去邦喬飛的演唱會。

▶ I want to see Black Eyed Peas.
  我想去黑眼豆豆的演唱會。

▶ I don't want to miss their concert.
  我不想錯過他們的演唱會。

▶ **It would be a shame** to miss out Lady Gaga.
  錯過女神卡卡就太可惜了。

> It would be a shame 表示「太可惜」的意思。

Let's go check out tickets. ◀ *Track 746*

我們去看有沒有票。

▶ Let's go see if there are tickets left.
  我們去看看還有沒有票。

▶ I'll go ask about tickets. 我去問問售票情形。

▶ I'll go get tickets. 我去買票。

I can't get a ticket for Broadway shows. ◀ *Track 747*

百老匯的票都買不到。

▶ All tickets are **sold out**. 所有的票都賣光了。

▶ Today's tickets are **sold out**. 今天的票都賣光光了。

> sold out 表示「賣光」的意思。

We need to dress formally. ◀ *Track 748*

我們必須穿著正式。

▶ I **dressed up** for today's concert.
  我為了今天的音樂會盛裝打扮。

▶ She really **dressed up** for today's event.
  為了今天的盛會,她特別盛裝打扮。

> dress up 表示「盛裝打扮」的意思。

Encore!

Track 749

再來一曲！

▶ Bravo!
　太棒了！

▶ Excellent!
　棒極了！

- -

I'd like to see another performance.

Track 750

我想再看別的表演。

▶ I want to see another one.
　我想再看一齣別的。

▶ Are you interested in another one?
　你對別齣有沒有興趣啊？

- -

Let's go get a drink.

Track 751

我們去點杯飲料。

▶ I'd like a gin tonic.
　我要一杯琴東尼。

▶ I'll have a beer.
　我要一瓶啤酒。

▶ Irish coffee for me.
　我要一杯愛爾蘭咖啡。

你可以這樣問

What's it made of?

◀ Track 752

這是什麼做的？

▶ **What kind of material is this?**
這是哪一種材質？

▶ **Is it durable?** 這耐用嗎？

> durable 表示「經久的、耐用的」的意思。

Can I have a look?

◀ Track 753

我可以看一下嗎？

▶ **Can I open this?** 我可以打開嗎？

▶ **Can I check what's inside?**
我可以看一下裡面是什麼嗎？

▶ **Can I take a closer look?**
我可以看仔細一點嗎？

Is this the local price?

◀ Track 754

這是當地的價錢嗎？

▶ **I think that might be the price for tourists.**
我覺得那可能是賣觀光客的價錢。

▶ **I think you can make it cheaper.**
我覺得可以便宜一點。

Do you have anything larger?

◀ Track 755

有沒有大一點的？

▶ **Do you have a bigger size?**
有大號的嗎？

▶ **I need a larger one.** 我需要大一點的。

How much is it in kilograms?

Track 756

這算公斤怎麼賣？

▶ What's that weight in kilograms?
這換成公斤有多重？

▶ Can I have a pound of those?
我要買一磅。

What's the weight? 用來詢問東西「有多重？」的意思。

Can I have half that amount?

Track 757

我能不能買那樣的一半？

▶ Can I have more? 我還要多一點好嗎？

▶ Can I have half of it? 我只要一半可以嗎？

Could you wrap this for me?

Track 758

可以幫我包裝嗎？

▶ Please wrap this for me. 請幫我包裝。

▶ I'd like to have it wrapped.
請幫我包裝起來。

▶ It's a gift. 是要送人的。

wrap 表示「包裝、包裹」的意思。

Could you deliver this to Taiwan?

Track 759

這可以送貨到台灣嗎？

▶ Can I have it delivered to Taiwan?
可以送到台灣嗎？

▶ I need it delivered.
我需要送貨。

▶ Do you provide a delivery service?
有提供送貨服務嗎？

Do you have anything to protect this?

◀ Track 760

有東西能保護這樣物品嗎？

▶ Be careful! It's fragile. 小心！物品易碎。
▶ Please wrap it carefully. 請仔細的包裝。
▶ Please be careful with it.
請小心！
▶ Please handle with care.
拿取請小心。

> fragile 表示「易
> 碎、易損壞」的
> 意思。

Is delivery included?

◀ Track 761

有包含送貨嗎？

▶ Could you send this to my hotel?
可以幫我送到旅館嗎？
▶ Is it possible to send it to this address?
能不能送到這個地址呢？
▶ Please send to this address.
請送到這個地址。

How much will it cost to send to the U.K.?

◀ Track 762

寄到英國要多少錢？

▶ How much does the delivery cost?
送貨要多少錢？
▶ What's the delivery charge?
送貨怎麼收費？
▶ How much should I pay?
我要付多少錢？

Do I need to sign anything?
◀ Track 763

我需要簽什麼嗎？
▶ Does it have to be signed for?
需要簽收嗎？
▶ I'll sign here. 我就簽在這裡。
▶ I'll put my signature here.
我簽名簽在這裡。

> sign 當動詞表示「簽名」的意思，而 sign for 則表示「簽收」的意思。

> signature 是名詞的「簽名」。

How long will it take to arrive?
◀ Track 764

多久會收到？
▶ Can you tell me the delivery date?
可以告訴我送貨日嗎？
▶ When will it be delivered? 什麼時候會送貨？
▶ What time of the day will it be delivered?
早中晚哪個時段會送到？

> What time of the day 就是詢問「在一天之中哪一個時段」的意思。

Can I get a refund?
◀ Track 765

可以退錢嗎？
▶ Can I get my money back? 我能退錢嗎？
▶ I want my money back. 我要退錢。
▶ Is it possible to get a refund?
有可能退錢嗎？

> get money back 表示「退費、把錢拿回來」的意思。

Do you have postcards?
◀ Track 766

你有賣明信片嗎？
▶ Are postcards sold here? 這裡有賣明信片嗎？
▶ Where can I find postcards? 哪裡找得到明信片？
▶ Do you have any other kinds? 還有其他的樣式嗎？

What are the specialties here?
🔊 *Track 767*

這裡有什麼特產？
▶ I'm looking for locally made souvenirs.
　我在找本地製的紀念品。
▶ I'm looking for souvenirs from this area.
　我在找這裡特產的紀念品。
▶ Are they made here? 這些是本地製的嗎？
▶ Are they made locally? 這些是本地製的嗎？

Are these handmade?
🔊 *Track 768*

這些是手工做的嗎？
▶ Is this handmade? 這是手工做的嗎？
▶ Did you make this? 這是你做的嗎？

What's the most popular gift?
🔊 *Track 769*

哪種禮物最熱門？
▶ What do most people buy? 大部分人都會買什麼？
▶ What's the best seller? 賣最好的是什麼？
▶ What do you recommend? 你推薦什麼？
▶ What would you choose? 你會挑什麼呢？

best seller 表示「銷售冠軍」的意思。

Are there other styles?
🔊 *Track 770*

有其他的樣式嗎？
▶ Are there other colors? 有其他的顏色嗎？
▶ Do you have more of the yellow one?
　黃色的還有沒有更多貨？
▶ Do you have any more in this range?
　這個系列還有沒有其他的？

range 表示「一系列」的意思。

Chapter 06 逛街購物

Do you have anything for kids?
Track 771
有適合小朋友的東西嗎？
- I'm looking for a gift for my son. 我在找送我兒子的禮物。
- I'm looking for something for my 5-year-old niece. 我在找送我五歲小姪女的禮物。

Could you wrap this for me?
Track 772
可以幫我包起來嗎？

> gift-wrap 表示「用包裝紙包裝起來」的意思。

- Could you gift-wrap this? 請幫我包成禮物好嗎？
- I'd like to have them wrapped. 請幫我包起來。
- They are for my family and friends. 這是要送家人朋友的。

Is this duty-free?
Track 773
這免稅嗎？
- Is this duty-free price? 這是免稅價嗎？
- It is much cheaper here. 這裡便宜多了。

How can I get a VAT refund?
Track 774
要怎樣辦退購物稅？

> VAT 代表的是 value added tax 就是「附加稅」的意思。

- How do I apply for a VAT refund? 我要怎麼退購物稅？
- What do I need to prepare for a VAT refund? 辦退稅要準備什麼？
- What should I bring? 要帶什麼東西？
- Will I have to wait long? 要等很久嗎？

238

How long will it take?

Track 775

要多久呢？

▶ How long does the process take? 退稅程序要多久？

▶ When will I get the refund?
我什麼時候可以領到退稅呢？

▶ How soon will I get the refund? 多快可以領到退稅呢？

> process 表示「處理過程、程序」的意思。

Can I claim a VAT refund on this? *Track 776*

這可以申請退附加稅嗎？

▶ I'd like to claim a VAT refund. 我要申請退附加稅。

▶ How do I claim a VAT refund? 我要怎麼申請退附加稅？

▶ Am I entitled to a VAT refund?
我符合退附加稅的資格嗎？

> claim 表示「申請、要求」的意思。

> be entitled to 表示「符合……資格、有……權力」的意思。

How much can I get?

Track 777

可以退多少錢？

▶ How much is my refund? 我的退稅有多少錢？

▶ How much is the refund? 能退多少錢？

▶ Can you tell me how much I'll get?
你能告訴我會領到多少錢嗎？

你可以這樣說

That's a bargain.

Track 778

撿到便宜了。

▶ I think you got a bargain. 我覺得你賺到了。

▶ That seems a good deal. 看起來滿划算的。

> bargain 表示「便宜貨」的意思。

It's a bit tight.

Track 779

這有點緊。

▶ It's a bit tight around the waist.　腰的地方有點緊。

▶ I can't squeeze in.　我穿不下去。

• •

It's too baggy.

Track 780

baggy 表示
「寬鬆」的
意思。

這太寬鬆了。

▶ It's way too large.　這太大了啦。

▶ It's much too large.　這大太多了。

• •

I don't know my size.

Track 781

我不知道我的尺寸。

▶ I'm not sure about my size.　我不確定我的尺寸。

▶ Do you know what this is in U.S. sizes?
你知道這是美國尺碼的幾號嗎？

• •

I don't need a bag.

Track 782

我不要袋子。

▶ I already have a bag.　我自己有袋子。

▶ I can put it in my bag.　我可以把那個放在我的袋子裡。

• •

I'd like to exchange this.

Track 783

我要換貨。

▶ May I exchange this?　我可以換貨嗎？

▶ I'm here for an exchange.
我是來換貨的。

• •

This item is damaged.

Track 784

這個貨品有損壞。

▶ It's broken. 東西壞掉了。

▶ It doesn't work. 根本不能用。

▶ There is a fault with it. 這東西有瑕疵。

> fault 表示「毛病、缺點、錯誤」的意思。

I'm looking for souvenirs.

Track 785

我在找紀念品。

▶ I want to go look for a souvenir.
以後看到找找看有沒有紀念品。

▶ There is a souvenir shop. 那裡有一家紀念品店。

▶ Let's go have a look at the souvenir shop.
我們去紀念品店看看。

> look for 是「尋找」的意思。

> souvenir 是「紀念品」的意思。

This will really remind me of this trip.

Track 786

這會讓我想起這趟旅行。

▶ I'll think of this trip when seeing this.
以後看到這個我就會想起這趟旅行。

▶ This will be a great souvenir.
這會是很好的紀念品。

> remind someone of something 表示「令某人想起某事」的意思。

Here are all my receipts.

Track 787

我的收據都在這裡。

▶ Here are the receipts. 收據都在這裡。

▶ I'll show you the receipts. 我給你看收據。

▶ Do you need to see the receipts? 需要看收據嗎？

Please send me a check.
Track 788

請寄支票給我。

▶ Can you send the refund as a check?
退稅可以寄支票嗎？

▶ Can I get cash? 可以退現金嗎？

▶ Can I have it refunded to my bank account?
可以退到我的戶頭嗎？

bank account
表示「銀行戶
頭」的意思。

Here are my bank account details.
Track 789

這是我的銀行帳號。

▶ Here is my address. 這是我的地址。

▶ This is my mailing address. 這是我的郵寄地址。

▶ Please send it to this address. 請寄到這個地址。

mailing
address 表示
「郵寄地址」
的意思。

Here is my passport.
Track 790

這是我的護照。

▶ Let me get my passport. 我找一下護照。

▶ Here it is. 在這裡。

▶ I got it. 找到了。

Thank you for your help.
Track 791

感謝你的協助。

▶ You've been a great help. 你幫了我大忙。

▶ That was very helpful. 真是太有幫助了。

helpful 表示
「有幫助的、
有益的」的
意思。

你可以這樣問

Do you really eat that?

Track 792

你們真的會吃那個嗎？

▶ **Are you serious?** 真的嗎？

▶ **No kidding!** 不是在開玩笑吧！

▶ **No way!** 不會吧！

・・・・・・・・・・・・・・・・・・・・・・・・・

Are there any good restaurants around here?

Track 793

這附近有好吃的餐廳嗎？

▶ **Any good restaurants near here?**
附近有好吃的餐廳嗎？

▶ **Any nice restaurants nearby?** 附近有不錯的餐廳嗎？

▶ **Any nice eateries around?** 附近有不錯的小吃店嗎？

> eatery 表示「小飯館」的意思，類似於國內的小吃店。

・・・・・・・・・・・・・・・・・・・・・・・・・

Would you recommend a good restaurant?

Track 794

請推薦一家好餐廳好嗎？

▶ **Any restaurants you recommend?**
你有沒有推薦的餐廳？

▶ **How's the restaurant across the street?**
對面那家餐廳怎麼樣？

・・・・・・・・・・・・・・・・・・・・・・・・・

Do I need to make a reservation?

Track 795

我必須先訂位嗎？

▶ **Do I need to book a table?** 我需要訂桌位嗎？

book / reserve / make a reservation 皆表示「訂位」的意思。

dress code 表示「穿著的規定和限制」，除了參加派對以前要詢問以外，有些高級餐館或宴會都會有穿著的要求。最好事先詢問，以免到場貽笑大方。

▶ **Do I need to reserve a table before we go?**
我們去之前需要先訂桌位嗎？

▶ **Should I book in advance?**
我需不需要事先訂位？

Is there any dress code?

Track 796

有穿著上的限制嗎？

▶ **Do I have to wear a tie?**
我一定要打領帶嗎？

▶ **Can I go in T-shirt and jeans?**
我可以穿 T 恤和牛仔褲去嗎？

When do you serve dinner until?

Track 797

你們晚餐供應到幾點？

▶ **What time does the kitchen close?**
廚房幾點休息？

▶ **When do you close?** 你們幾點打烊？

What's that dish over there?

Track 798

那邊那道菜是什麼？

▶ **What's the name of the dish that lady is having?**
請問那位女士在用的菜叫什麼？

▶ **Would you tell me what's it like?**
請告訴我那道菜是什麼樣的？

▶ **Will you tell me what kind of dish it is?**
請告訴我那是什麼樣的一道菜？

Do you have a menu in English?

Track 799

請問有英文的菜單嗎？

▶ Is there an English menu? 有英文的菜單嗎？
▶ Is there a menu in Chinese? 有中文的菜單嗎？
▶ Do you have a Chinese menu? 請問有中文的菜單嗎？

What do you recommend?

Track 800

你推薦什麼？

▶ What's your house special? 你們的招牌菜是什麼？
▶ Anything special? 有沒有什麼特別的料理？
▶ What's the specialty here? 這裡的招牌菜是什麼？

> house special
> 或 specialty 表示
> 各餐廳的「招牌
> 菜」。

What kind of desserts do you have today?

Track 801

今天有什麼樣的甜點？

▶ What are our choices? 我們有什麼選擇？
▶ What are the choices for dessert?
甜點有什麼選擇？
▶ Do you have any hot desserts?
有沒有熱的甜點？

Do you take credit cards?

Track 802

你們收信用卡嗎？

▶ I'd like to pay by credit card.
我要用信用卡付帳。
▶ I'll pay with cash. 我付現金。
▶ Please split our bill. 請幫我們分開算。
▶ It's on me! 我請客！

> 要說「我請客」
> 除了 It's on me.
> 也可以說 My
> treat.

Can I have some napkins?

◀ Track 803

給我一些餐巾紙好嗎?

(paper) napkin 是「餐巾紙」, 但往往可以 省略 paper 不說。

▶ Please give me some napkins. 請給我一些餐巾紙。

▶ Where can I find napkins? 哪裡有餐巾紙?

Does salad come with the dish?

◀ Track 804

有隨餐附沙拉嗎?

come with 表 示「伴隨而 來」的意思。

▶ I'd like to have a side salad. 我想點附餐沙拉。

▶ I'd like to have fries on the side. 附餐我要點薯條。

▶ I'll have the potato salad. 我要選洋芋沙拉。

Could I have more water, please?

◀ Track 805

請幫我加水。

▶ Would you bring us another glass of water?
可以再給我們一杯水嗎?

▶ Would you bring us two spoons, please?
請幫我們拿兩支湯匙好嗎?

Would you bring us the pepper, please?

◀ Track 806

請幫我們拿胡椒。

▶ Please bring us the salt. 請幫我們拿鹽。

▶ Please give me some chili powder.
請給我一些辣椒粉。

▶ May I have the vinegar?
請幫我拿醋。

Are there any tables upstairs? ◀ *Track 807*

樓上有位子嗎？

▶ Do you have more seats downstairs?
　樓下有其他位子嗎？

▶ Is this table taken?
　這張桌子有人嗎？

▶ Is anybody sitting here?
　這裡有人坐嗎？

> Is this table / seat taken? 是在看到有位子但不確定時用來詢問「該位子有沒有人」的意思。

你可以這樣說

There are so many things I want to try. ◀ *Track 808*

好多東西我都想嚐嚐看。

▶ I want to try the local food.
　我想吃吃看當地的食物。

▶ Let's try something special tonight.
　我們今晚來吃些特別的。

▶ There are a lot of herbs in this dish.
　這道菜裡面有許多香料。

I have to order one for myself. ◀ *Track 809*

我得自己點一份餐點。

▶ They don't share food here.
　這裡的人不會吃對方的食物。

▶ They are not used to sharing food.
　他們不習慣大家分食。

▶ You'd better eat from your own plate.
　你最好吃自己盤子裡的食物就好。

I'm not sure if I dare to try crickets. ◀ *Track 810*
我不確定我敢吃蟋蟀。
▶ That's not for me. 敬謝不敏。
▶ I really can't. 我真的不敢啦。
▶ I'll have a small bite.
　我吃一小口。

> have a bite 表示「吃一口」的意思。

I'll try to eat with my hand. ◀ *Track 811*
我也試著用手吃飯看看。
▶ Can you give me some tips?
　可以告訴我一些訣竅嗎？
▶ Would you teach me how to eat with my hand?
　請教我怎麼用手吃飯好嗎？
▶ Can I use both hands? 我可以用兩手嗎？
▶ Can I use my left hand to help?
　我可以用左手幫忙嗎？

> tip 除了指「小費」，在此表示「訣竅」的意思。

There is no pork served here. ◀ *Track 812*
這裡都沒有豬肉的餐點呢。
▶ Pork is not sold here. 這裡沒有賣豬肉。
▶ I miss pork chops, but well...
　我好想念豬排喔，但是……好吧。
▶ Muslims don't eat pork. 回教徒不吃豬肉的。

> Muslim 是「回教」或「回教徒」的意思。

I'm not used to knives and forks. ◀ *Track 813*
我真不習慣用刀叉。
▶ I'm not good at using knives and forks.
　我刀叉用得不太好。

Let's try some buttered tea. ◀ *Track 814*

我們也試試看酥油茶吧。

▶ The pad thai is so tasty. 這個泰式炒河粉超好吃。

▶ What's in Gulasch? 匈牙利牛肉湯裡有什麼？

▶ Wow! I love falafel and hummus.
哇！我超愛炸豆餅和鷹嘴豆泥。

falafel 和 hummus 都是常見的中東菜色。

I'd like to make a reservation. ◀ *Track 815*

我想要訂位。

▶ I'd like to reserve a table. 我想要訂一桌。

▶ I'd like to reserve for two.
我想要訂兩個人的位子。

▶ I'd like to book a table for ten.
我想要訂一桌十個人。

如欲說明訂位人數，則在 book、reserve 和 make areservation 後加上 for 後面再加上人數。

I'd like to book a table for seven tonight. ◀ *Track 816*

我想訂今晚七點的位子。

▶ I'd like to book for two for lunch tomorrow.
我想訂兩個明天午餐的位子。

▶ Do you still have seats for Saturday?
請問禮拜六還有位子嗎？

I'll have the beefsteak. ◀ *Track 817*

我要牛排。

▶ I'll have the same. 我也一樣。

▶ Same here. 一樣。

▶ I'll have the fish fillet. 我要魚排。

This is not what we ordered.

🔊 *Track 818*

這不是我們點的。

▶ I don't think this is what I ordered.
　這應該不是我點的。

▶ Is this what I ordered?
　這是我點的嗎？

It tastes really good.

🔊 *Track 819*

真的很好吃。

▶ It's so yummy.　超好吃的。

▶ This is so delicious.　好美味喔。

▶ It's not my type of food.　這不合我的口味。

I'd like to have a beer.

🔊 *Track 820*

我想來一瓶啤酒。

▶ Can I have another beer?　我要再來一瓶啤酒。

▶ I'd like to have another glass of red wine.
　我要再來一杯紅酒。

soft drinks
指的是「不含
酒精的軟性飲
料」。

▶ What kind of soft drinks do you have?
　你們有什麼不含酒精的飲料？

I feel like a dessert.

🔊 *Track 821*

我想吃甜點。

▶ I want to have something sweet.　我想吃點甜的。

▶ Let's order some desserts.　我們來點甜點吧。

▶ We'd like to see the dessert menu.
　我們想看甜點的菜單。

We'll share one cheese cake. 🔊 *Track 822*

我們要分一個起司蛋糕。

▶ Chocolate brownie for me. 我要巧克力布朗尼。

▶ I'd like two scoops of ice cream, one strawberry and one vanilla. 我要兩球冰淇淋，一球草莓和一球香草。

▶ I'll skip the dessert. 我不吃甜點了。

> skip 表示「跳過」的意思，跳過食物即為「不吃」或「沒吃」的意思。

I'd like a cup of tea with milk. 🔊 *Track 823*

我要一杯奶茶。

▶ Can I have a coffee? 我要一杯咖啡。

▶ One espresso, please. 請給我一杯濃縮咖啡。

▶ One cappuccino for me and one latte for my wife. 請給我一杯卡布奇諾，我太太要一杯拿鐵。

No sugar for my coffee. 🔊 *Track 824*

我的咖啡不要加糖。

▶ I don't want any sugar. 我不要加糖。

▶ I want black coffee, please. 請給我黑咖啡。

▶ Please don't put any sugar in my coffee. 我的咖啡不要加糖。

Please pack the leftovers for us. 🔊 *Track 825*

請幫我們打包剩菜。

▶ I'd like to take the leftover home. 我要把剩菜打包回去。

▶ Do you have a doggie bag? 你們有沒有打包剩菜的袋子？

▶ Can I have a doggie bag? 請給我一個打包剩菜的袋子好嗎？

> leftover 表示「剩菜」的意思。

> doggie bag 是餐廳提供客人打包未吃完剩菜回去的袋子。

The bill, please!

Track 826

買單！

▶ Please give us the bill. 請給我們帳單。

▶ Please bring me the check. 請給我帳單。

漢堡的種類有很多，在 burger 前面加上肉的種類就可以表示要吃的漢堡，如：fish burger「魚堡」/ chickenburger「雞肉堡」或 cheese burger「起士堡」等。

One hamburger, please.

Track 827

請給我一份漢堡。

▶ One chicken burger, please.
請給我一份香雞堡。

▶ Two veggie burgers.
兩個素食漢堡。

I'll have a Meal 2.

Track 828

我要一個二號餐。

set meal 就是已經搭配好的「套餐」。

▶ One Meal 2 and one Meal 5. 一個二號餐和一個五號餐。

▶ Two Set A, please. 請給我們兩個 A 套餐。

▶ Do you have any set meals? 請問有沒有套餐？

One small orange juice, please.

Track 829

請給我一杯小杯柳橙汁。

with ice 是「加冰」，with no ice 就是「不加冰」。

▶ Two large cokes, with no ice. 兩杯大杯可樂，去冰。

▶ Do you have milk? 這裡有賣牛奶嗎？

I'd like a large serving of French fries.

Track 830

我想要一份大份薯條。

▶ **Two large fries, please.** 兩份大份薯條。
▶ **Where is the ketchup?** 蕃茄醬在哪裡？
▶ **Please give me two packages of ketchup.**
　 請給我兩包蕃茄醬。

> ketchup 就是沾
> 食薯條常用的
> 「番茄醬」。

I'll eat it here.
　　　　　　　　　　　　　　　　　▶ *Track 831*
我要在這裡吃。
▶ **We'll dine in here.** 我們要在裡面用。
▶ **For here.** 要內用。

I'll take it out.
　　　　　　　　　　　　　　　　　▶ *Track 832*
我要帶走。
▶ **For take away.** 要外帶的。
▶ **To go.** 要外帶。

You forgot about our apple pie.
　　　　　　　　　　　　　　　　　▶ *Track 833*
你忘記我們的蘋果派了。
▶ **We didn't get the apple pie.**
　 我們沒拿到蘋果派喔。
▶ **We ordered a fruit salad but haven't got it.**
　 我們點了一個水果沙拉但是還沒來。
▶ **Can you check with the kitchen for our fish burger?**
　 可以跟廚房確認一下我們的魚排堡好了嗎？

緊急求助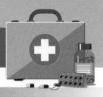

你可以這樣問

Where is the nearest pharmacy?
Track 834

最近的藥局在哪裡？

▶ **Do you know where I can get some medicine?**
你知道哪裡可以買到藥嗎？

▶ **I need some painkillers.** 我需要止痛藥。

painkiller 是
「止痛藥」的
意思。

▶ **Where can I find medical assistance?**
哪裡可以找到醫療協助？

Do you have anything for a fever?
Track 835

有沒有退燒藥？

▶ **Does this help relieve stomach pains?**
這可以舒緩胃部疼痛嗎？

▶ **I need something to help me sleep.**
我需要助眠的東西。

▶ **I can't sleep at night.** 我晚上睡不著。

▶ **What do you recommend?** 你有沒有推薦什麼呢？

Can you call me a doctor?
Track 836

能幫我請醫生嗎？

▶ **Where is the nearest medical center?**
最近的診所在哪裡？

▶ **Where can I find a doctor?** 哪裡找的到醫生？

How long until the new passport arrives?
Track 837

新護照要多久才會好？

replacement
表示「補發、
替代品」的
意思。

▶ **When will the replacement arrive?** 補發什麼時候會好？

▶ Does that mean I can't leave the country for now?
這是不是表示我暫時不能離開這個國家？

Can I get it sooner?
▪ *Track 838*

可以快一點辦好嗎？

▶ Should I pay extra? 我要另外付費嗎？
▶ What's the fee? 費用多少？
▶ What's the cost? 費用多少？

Will you put me on another plane?
▪ *Track 839*

可以幫我安排其他飛機嗎？

▶ Will you arrange other transport for me?
能幫我安排其他交通工具嗎？
▶ How will you get me there? 你要怎麼把我送達目的地？

What is the problem?
▪ *Track 840*

是什麼問題呢？

▶ What is holding us up? 是什麼害我們耽誤了？
▶ What is the cause of the delay? 誤點是什麼原因？
▶ Why have we stopped? 我為什麼停下來？

> hold up 表示「阻礙、攔截」的意思。

Is there another way to get there?
▪ *Track 841*

還有別的路嗎？

▶ Is there a faster alternative? 有快一點的其他路線嗎？
▶ Can I get on another train? 我可以改搭另一班火車嗎？
▶ Will we still arrive on time? 我們還會準時抵達嗎？

> alternative 表示「供選擇的其他辦法」。

Is it quicker to walk?

Track 842

走路會不會比較快？

▶ I'll get off and walk from here. 我要下車從這裡用走的。

▶ Is it quicker to go by a taxi? 搭計程車會不會快一點？

Can I claim compensation?

Track 843

我可以求償嗎？

▶ Can I get my money back? 可以退費嗎？

▶ Will you pay for accomodation?
你們會為我付住宿費嗎？

When will it leave?

Track 844

什麼時候會開呢？

▶ What's the new expected arrival time?
新的預計抵達時間是什麼時候？

▶ How long must we wait? 我們還要等多久？

▶ How much longer will it take? 還需要多久的時間？

Where am I?

Track 845

我在哪裡啊？

▶ Where are we? 我們在哪裡啊？

▶ I think I'm lost. 我想我迷路了。

▶ I think we are lost. 我想我們迷路了。

What is the name of this street?

Track 846

這條街叫什麼名字？

▶ Are we on Thatcher Street? 我們在柴契爾街上嗎？

▶ Do you know this area? 你對這一帶熟悉嗎？
▶ Have you heard of a restaurant called Green Parrot? 你有聽過一間餐廳叫「綠鸚鵡」嗎？

hear of 表示「聽過」的意思。

Can you show me on a map?　◀ Track 847
可否請你在地圖上指出來？
▶ Do you have a map? 你有沒有地圖？
▶ Where are we on the map? 我們在地圖上的哪裡？
▶ We are trying to reach here. 我們想要去到這裡。

Can you give me directions?　◀ Track 848
你可以幫我指路嗎？
▶ Can you help me find the science museum?
　你可以幫我找自然科學博物館在哪裡嗎？
▶ Do you know where I can find a map?
　你知道哪裡有地圖嗎？
▶ Please show me. 請指給我看。

direction 表示「方向」的意思。

Can you point me to the beach?.　◀ Track 849
你可以指給我看往海灘的路嗎？
▶ Are we near the City Hall?
　我們離市政府近不近？
▶ How do I get to the Central Train Station?
　我要怎麼去中央車站？
▶ Which way should I go?
　我要走哪個方向？

Are we driving in the right direction?

Track 850

我們開這個方向對嗎？

▶ **Where do we turn off?** 要在哪裡轉彎啊？
▶ **Take the next left.** 下一條左轉。
▶ **Turn right at the next traffic light.** 下一個紅綠燈右轉。

Can you write that down?

Track 851

可以請你寫下來嗎？

▶ **Can you draw me a map?** 可以畫個地圖給我看嗎？
▶ **Can you tell the taxi driver?** 可以告訴計程車司機嗎？
▶ **Can you show me which bus I need?**
可以告訴我需要搭哪一班公車嗎？

Can you tell me how to get to my hotel?

Track 852

可以告訴我怎麼去我的旅館嗎？

▶ **How should I get to my hotel?** 我要怎麼去我的旅館？
▶ **How far is my hotel from here?**
從這裡到我的旅館有多遠？
▶ **How long does it take to get there?**
多久可以到那裡？

Is it in this direction?

Track 853

是往這個方向嗎？

▶ **Is this the way?** 這條路對嗎？
▶ **Am I going the right way?** 我這樣走對嗎？

Can we get a band-aid?

🔊 *Track 854*

可以給我們一個 **OK** 繃嗎？

▶ Do you have any bandages? 有沒有繃帶？

▶ Do you have a first-aid kit? 有急救箱嗎？

▶ Do you know first-aid? 你會不會急救處理？

> band-aid 是「OK
> 繃」的意思。

> first-aid-kit 是「急
> 救箱」的意思。

Are you OK?

🔊 *Track 855*

你還好嗎？

▶ Are you hurt anywhere? 你有沒有哪裡受傷？

▶ Do you need help? 需要幫忙嗎？

▶ Do you want me to call the doctor? 需要我叫醫生嗎？

▶ Please call an ambulance. 請叫救護車。

Can I have a copy of the police report?

🔊 *Track 856*

報案紀錄可以印一份給我嗎？

▶ Can I have the police report number?
可以給我報案紀錄號碼嗎？

▶ Can you make a copy for me? 可以幫我影印一份嗎？

▶ What happens next? 接下來怎麼辦？

Who do I turn to for help?

🔊 *Track 857*

我要找誰幫我？

▶ Who can help me? 誰能幫我？

▶ Where can I find help? 哪裡能幫我？

▶ Where is the embassy? 大使館在哪裡？

> turn to 表示
> 「求助、轉向」
> 的意思。

你可以這樣說

I'm feeling ill.
Track 858

我人不舒服。

▶ I'm not feeling well. 我不太舒服。

▶ I've got a high temperature. 我發燒了。

▶ I may need to see a doctor. 我可能需要看醫生。

> have / get a high temperature 有個很高的溫度，表示「發燒」的意思。

My stomach hurts.
Track 859

我的胃不舒服。

▶ I have a stomachache. 我胃痛。

▶ I think I ate something bad. 我想我吃到壞掉的東西了。

▶ I may have food poisoning. 我可能食物中毒了。

> food poisoning 表示「食物中毒」的意思。

It hurts here.
Track 860

這裡會痛。

▶ I feel pain here. 我這裡會痛。

▶ My head aches. 我頭痛。

▶ My arm hurts. 我的手臂疼痛。

She may need medical attention.
Track 861

她可能需要醫療照護。

▶ He's had a serious accident. 他出了嚴重的意外。

▶ I think you should get examined.
我覺得你應該去接受檢查。

> get examined 表示「接受檢查」的意思。

I have a toothache.
Track 862

我牙痛。

▶ I need a dentist. 我需要看牙醫。
▶ I have a loose tooth. 我有一顆牙齒鬆動。
▶ I have a loose filling. 我補牙的地方快掉了。

> filling 表示補牙的「填補物」的意思。

I'm feeling much better now.
Track 863

我現在好多了。

▶ That has helped a lot. 那個很有幫助。
▶ The symptoms have gone. 症狀都消失了。

> symptom 表示「症狀」的意思。

I can't find my passport.
Track 864

我找不到我的護照。

▶ I've lost my ID card. 我的身份證掉了。
▶ My credit card is missing. 我的信用卡不見了。
▶ Where are my plane tickets? 我的機票呢？

I need to report a lost passport.
Track 865

我要掛失護照。

▶ How can I get a new one? 要怎樣辦新的？
▶ I must call my embassy. 我必須打電話給大使館。

> embassy 是「大使館」的意思。

I need a new set of tickets.
Track 866

我需要開新的票。

▶ My plane tickets need replacing. 我需要補發機票。
▶ Can you issue me new ones? 可以幫我重新開票嗎？
▶ Is there a travel agency nearby? 附近有旅行社嗎？

> issue 表示「開票、核發、發行」的意思。

I lost the original.

🔊 *Track 867*

我的正本掉了。

▶ Here is a copy. 這裡有印本。

▶ I'm waiting for a replacement. 我在等補發。

▶ My new passport shall arrive soon.
  我的新護照應該快送來了。

I have my driver's license.

🔊 *Track 868*

我有駕照。

▶ I have my student card. 我有學生證。

▶ I have my passport number. 我有我的護照號碼。

▶ I have my itinerary. 我有行程表。

I need to cancel my credit card.

🔊 *Track 869*

我要取消我的信用卡。

▶ I need to report a lost credit card. 我要掛失信用卡。

▶ My credit card may have been stolen.
  我的信用卡可能被偷了。

▶ I need a new credit card. 我需要一張新的信用卡。

▶ Can you send a new one to my hotel?
  可以寄一張新卡到我的旅館嗎？

The flight is delayed.

🔊 *Track 870*

飛機誤點。

▶ The train is cancelled. 火車取消了。

▶ The train is diverted. 火車更改路線。

▶ We have to take a detour. 我們必須繞道。

▶ The bus is not running. 公車停駛。

detour 表示
「繞道、繞行」
的意思。

I will miss my connection.

Track 871

我會來不及轉車。

▶ What about my connecting flight?
我的接續班機怎麼辦？

▶ I have to transfer. 我必須轉機。

▶ I must arrive before 5 p.m. 我一定要在下午五點前抵達。

I need to call ahead.

Track 872

我必須打電話到下一站。

▶ Someone is expecting me. 有人在等我。

▶ I have an appointment. 我有預約。

▶ I will miss the meeting. 我要來不及開會了。

call ahead 表示
「打電話到下一
個地方」的意思，
在此打電話的對
象可能是餐廳、
旅館、接送服務
等已經預先安排
好的接續行程。

I crashed the car.

Track 873

我撞車了。

▶ I've been in a car accident. 我剛車禍。

▶ I had a car crash. 我撞車了。

▶ The car hit a tree. 車子撞上一棵樹。

I've cut myself.

Track 874

我自己割傷了。

▶ I'm bleeding. 我正在流血。

▶ I'm bruised. 我瘀青了。

▶ It looks worse than it is. 實際上沒那麼糟糕啦。

bruise 表示「瘀
青、青腫、碰傷」
的意思。

I can't walk.

🔊 *Track 875*

我不能走路。

▶ I can't move my arm.　我的手臂沒辦法移動。

▶ I can't feel my feet.　我的雙腳失去知覺。

▶ Can you stay with me?　你可以留下來陪我嗎？

I have a puncture.

🔊 *Track 876*

輪胎被刺到了。

> flat tire 表示
> 「爆胎」的
> 意思。

▶ I have a flat tire.　有個輪胎爆胎。

▶ The battery is flat.　電瓶沒電了。

▶ The battery is dead.　電池沒電了。

We are completely out of gas.

🔊 *Track 877*

我們完全沒有油了。

> gas station 是
> 「加油站」的
> 意思。

▶ We need to call a tow truck.　我們要打電話叫拖車。

▶ We need to find the nearest gas station.
　我們要找最近的加油站。

▶ We need to get a ride.　我們需要搭便車。

I'm locked out of my room.

🔊 *Track 878*

我被鎖在房間外面。

> pass key 表示
> 飯店內每一間
> 房都可開啟的
> 「萬用鑰匙」。

▶ Can you open the door for me?　可以幫我開門嗎？

▶ Do you have a pass key?　你有萬用鑰匙嗎？

Help! I've been robbed.

🔊 *Track 879*

救命！我被搶了。

▶ My wallet has been stolen.　我的皮夾被偷了。

▶ I've been mugged.
我遭到襲擊被搶了。

▶ My bag's been taken.
有人把我的袋子拿走了。

> mug 非常口語，表示「遭到襲擊並被搶劫」的意思。

Call the police!
◀ *Track 880*
快報警！

▶ Where is the police station? 警察局在哪裡？

▶ I want to report a robbery. 我要報案，是個搶案。

▶ I need to report an accident. 我要報案，發生了意外。

They stole my orange backpack.
◀ *Track 881*
他們偷了我的橘色背包。

▶ My passport was inside.
我的護照在裡面。

▶ There were two credit cards inside.
裡面有兩張信用卡。

▶ All my money was in there too.
我所有的錢也都在裡面。

It happened suddenly.
◀ *Track 882*
事情發生的很突然。

▶ I didn't see their faces.
我沒看到他們的臉。

▶ There were two of them.
他們一共有兩個人。

> suddenly 表示「突然地、意外地」的意思。

▶ They were wearing masks.
他們有帶面罩。

I'd like to make a claim.

Track 883

我要申請理賠。

▶ **Does my insurance cover this?**
我的保險有給付這個嗎？

▶ **My luggage has been stolen.**
我的行李被偷了。

▶ **I had a car accident.**
我出了車禍。

▶ **I was in hospital for three days.**
我住院住了三天。

It's an emergency.

Track 884

這是緊急事件。

▶ **My wife has to go to the hospital.**
我太太需要去醫院。

▶ **I need a doctor** as soon as possible.
我需要醫生，越快越好。

as soon as possible = ASAP 表示「越快越好」的意思。

I have a rash.

Track 885

我起疹子。

▶ **I have a** swelling.
我有個地方腫起來。

▶ **I was bitten by a snake.**
我被蛇咬了。

▶ **I was stung by an insect.**
我被蚊蟲叮咬。

swelling 表示「腫脹」的意思。

Special

貼心嚴選
出發前
必學情境

坐車、開車出門，出發前一定要知道

① **We're stuck in the traffic.**
我們塞在車陣中了。

. . . .

② **Is there a parking lot around here?**
這附近有停車場嗎？

. . . .

③ **I can't start the engine.**
我無法發動引擎。

. . . .

④ **Could you check the brakes for me?**
請你幫我檢查一下煞車好嗎？

. . . .

⑤ **I think there's something wrong with the transmission.**
我覺得車子的變速箱有問題。

. . . .

⑥ **I'm almost out of gas.**
車子快要沒油了。

. . . .

⑦ **I got a ticket for speeding.**
我收到一張超速罰單。

. . . .

8 **Watch out for speed traps around here.**
注意這附近的測速照相喔。

9 **It's getting dark. Turn on the headlights.**
天快黑了。把車頭燈打開吧。

10 **You forgot to give a turn signal.**
你忘了打方向燈了。

11 **The sign says you can't make a U-turn here.**
告示牌說你不能在這邊迴轉。

12 **Where does this bus go?**
這輛公車是往哪個方向？

13 **Excuse me! Where is the bus stop?**
請問一下！公車站在哪裡？

14 **Do I have to buy a ticket before getting on the bus?**
要在上車前先買票嗎？

⑮ **Can you tell me where to get off?**
請告訴我在哪裡下車好嗎？

. . . .

⑯ **Do I need to change lines?**
需要換線嗎？

. . . .

⑰ **When is the last bus?**
末班公車是幾點？

. . . .

⑱ **Does this bus go to the City Library?**
這輛公車有到市立圖書館嗎？

. . . .

⑲ **I want to book an HSR ticket online.**
我要上網訂一張高鐵票。

. . . .

⑳ **How long will it take by taxi?**
搭計程車要多久？

. . . .

搭飛機出國，
出發到機場前一定要知道：

① **I'd like to book a flight to New York.**
我想訂去紐約的機位。

. . . .

② **I'd like to book a one-way ticket.**
我要訂單程票。

③ **My reservation number is AZ6768.**
我的訂位號碼是 **AZ6768**。

④ **Is there any direct flight?**
有直飛的班機嗎？

⑤ **I need to book for special meals.**
我需要訂特殊餐點。

⑥ **Can I use my miles to upgrade my seat?**
可以用累積哩程升等座位嗎？

⑦ **I'd like to reconfirm my flight.**
我要再確認我的班機。

⑧ **Hi! I'd like to check in.**
你好，我要辦登機手續。

⑨ **Fill in the luggage tag.**
填一下行李吊牌。

⑩ **Can I change it to a later flight?**
可以改晚一點的班機嗎？

⑪ **The flight is delayed.**
飛機誤點。

⑫ **Can I get a window seat?**
我要靠窗的位子。

⑬ **May I change seats?**
我可以換座位嗎？

⑭ **I need a blanket.**
我需要一條毛毯。

⑮ **May I have a glass of water?**
我可以要一杯水嗎？

⑯ **What time will we arrive in Vancouver?**
我們幾點會到溫哥華？

⑰ **The purpose of my visit is sightseeing.**
我此行是為了觀光。

⑱ **Where can I find a baggage cart?**
哪裡有行李推車？

⑲ **The baggage claim area is this way.**
行李提領區往這邊。

⑳ I have nothing to declare.
我沒有東西需要申報。

逛街購物買衣服，出發前一定要知道

① I heard about a new store.
我聽說有一家新的店。

· ·

② The new mall has an opening sale.
新的購物中心有開幕優惠。

· ·

③ Do you like this kind or that kind?
你喜歡這款還是那款？

· ·

④ It comes in several colors.
它有許多顏色。

· ·

⑤ Can I try that one on too?
我可以也試那件嗎？

· ·

⑥ Does it make me look fat?
它會讓我看起來很胖嗎？

· ·

⑦ It doesn't fit.
它不合身。

· ·

⑧ Do you have anything larger?
有沒有大一點的？

- -

⑨ We can fix the size.
我們可以修改尺寸。

- -

⑩ I don't know my size.
我不知道我的尺寸。

- -

⑪ How much is this?
這個多少錢？

- -

⑫ Can I get a discount?
有沒有折扣啊？

- -

⑬ I don't see a price. How much is this?
這沒有標價，多少錢啊？

- -

⑭ Is this duty-free?
這免稅嗎？

- -

⑮ Can you wrap this for me?
可以幫我包裝嗎？

- -

⑯ Can you pack them separately?
可以幫我分開包嗎？

- -

⑰ **I'd like to return this.**
我想要退還這個。

⑱ **Can I get a refund?**
可以退錢嗎？

⑲ **I found a tear in the skirt.**
我發現裙子上有一個裂縫。

⑳ **What is your return policy?**
你們退換貨的規定是什麼？

「去上學，出發前一定要知道」

① **What's your favorite subject?**
你最喜歡的科目是什麼？

② **What major do you want to study in the future?**
你以後想唸什麼科系？

③ **Is your science class interesting?**
自然課好玩嗎？

4 I forgot to bring my homework to school today.
我今天忘記帶課本了。

5 I have tons of homework today!
我今天的功課超多的！

6 Do you like the new history teacher?
你喜歡新來的歷史老師嗎？

7 The placement exam will be held on next Monday.
分班考試測驗將於下週一舉行。

8 I have to study English grammar for tomorrow's quiz.
我必須準備明天的文法考試。

9 When's your mid-term exam?
你的期中考是什麼時候？

10 I got a bad grade on the final test.
我期末考考得很不好。

Special

貼心嚴選—出發前必學情境

⑪ **Did you take any notes in math class today?**
你今天在數學課有寫筆記嗎？

⑫ **Can I borrow your notebook?**
我可以借你的筆記嗎？

⑬ **I have highlighted some important points in the textbook.**
我在課本裡面有標些重點。

⑭ **Our group has some questions to discuss about this chapter.**
我們組對這章節有些問題。

⑮ **What do I need to apply for school loans?**
申請助學貸款需要什麼？

⑯ **How do you determine your *G.P.A.?**
如何計算你的 **G.P.A.?**

＊註解：Grade Point Average，學業成績平均，許多大學用此制度評估學生成績。

「去上班，出發前一定要知道」

① **I need to work overtime today.**
我今晚要加班。

❷ **The meeting will start in ten minutes.**
會議將在十分鐘後開始。

③ **I'd like to apply for some stationary.**
我想申請一些文具用品。

❹ **Would you please take a look at this report for me?**
可以幫我看這份文件嗎？

⑤ **We've run out of A4 paper.**
A4 紙用完了。

❻ **I support this proposal.**
我附議這個提案。

⑦ **The directors are going to discuss the matter again.**
主管們將再進行一次討論。

⑧ This is our new colleague.
這是我們的新同事。

⑨ I'll be in meetings all day today.
我今天有一整天的會。

⑩ What time is the meeting?
會議是從幾點開始？

⑪ Who's taking the minutes?
誰要做會議紀錄？

⑫ The meeting is going to be rescheduled.
會議必須要重新安排時間。

⑬ Would you walk me through the workflow?
可以麻煩你跟我講一下工作流程嗎？

⑭ I'm running late on my sales report.
我的業績報告要來不及了。

「去餐廳吃飯，出發前一定要知道」

① **What kind of food do you prefer?**
你偏好哪一類食物？

. . . .

❷ **Come on, the restaurant has a bad reputation.**
拜託，那家餐廳評價很差。

. . . .

③ **I'd like to make a reservation.**
我想要訂位。

. . . .

❹ **When are the opening hours?**
營業時間是？

. . . .

⑤ **When do you serve dinner until?**
你們晚餐供應到幾點？

. . . .

❻ **For here or to go?**
內用或外帶？

. . . .

⑦ **What do you recommend?**
你有任何推薦的餐點嗎？

. . . .

❽ **Do you have a Chinese menu?**
請問有中文菜單嗎？

. . . .

⑨ **I want a large French fries and a small coke, please.**
我要點一份大份薯條和一杯小杯可樂。

⑩ **I'll have mushroom sauce.**
我想要搭配蘑菇醬。

⑪ **I'd like a glass of juice.**
我要喝果汁。

⑫ **I want to have a piece of cheesecake after we eat.**
飯後我想來片起司蛋糕。

⑬ **I need something low fat and low caffeine.**
我需要一些低脂和低咖啡因的。

⑭ **Would you please pass me the pepper?**
請將胡椒遞給我。

⑮ **Can I have some napkins?**
給我一些餐巾紙好嗎？

⑯ **Sorry, I just spilt my coke.**
抱歉，我剛打翻了可樂。

⑰ **The chicken was too salty.**
這雞肉太鹹了。

. . . .

⑱ **You are serving the wrong order.**
你送錯餐了。

. . . .

⑲ **You forgot about our apple pie.**
你忘記我們的蘋果派了。

. . . .

⑳ **Please pack the leftovers for us.**
請幫我們打包剩菜。

住旅館或在外租房子，出發前一定要知道

① **I'd like to make a reservation.**
我要訂房。

. . . .

② **Do you have a double room free?**
還有雙人房嗎？

. . . .

③ **How much does it cost for one night?**
住一個晚上要多少錢？

. . . .

④ **Is breakfast included?**
有包含早餐嗎？

⑤ **What time is check out?**
幾點要退房？

⑥ **Which floor is it on?**
房間在幾樓？

⑦ **Do you have a safe?**
有保險箱嗎？

⑧ **Is there a laundry service?**
有送洗服務嗎？

⑨ **Is there a gym?**
有健身房嗎？

⑩ **Can I order room service?**
我可以叫客房服務嗎？

⑪ **There is no hot water.**
根本沒有熱水。

⑫ **I need a hair dryer.**
我需要吹風機。

⑬ **I need an extra pillow.**
我還需要一個枕頭。

⑭ **The air conditioning is not working.**
空調壞掉了。

⑮ **My sheets need to be changed.**
我的床單該換了。

⑯ **Where is the toothpaste?**
牙膏在哪裡？

⑰ **My toilet is stuck.**
我的馬桶塞住了。

⑱ **The rent includes water and the Internet fee.**
這房租包含水費和網路費。

⑲ **I'm looking for a female roommate.**
我在找一名女室友。

「外出運動、遊玩，出發前一定要知道」

① **What type of movies do you like?**
你喜歡哪種電影類型？

❷ **Is this movie dubbed?**
這部電影有上字幕嗎？

③ **The concert hall is so luxurious.**
音樂廳好豪華。

❹ **Two tickets, please.**
請給我兩張票。

⑤ **Can I get tickets at the box office?**
現場有售票嗎？

❻ **Can I return this ticket?**
我可以退票嗎？

⑦ **Is this musical still on?**
這部歌舞劇還在演嗎？

❽ **We need to dress formally.**
我們必須穿著正式。

⑨ **How long is the performance?**
表演全長多長？

⑩ **Don't drop the camera.**
照相機不要摔到。

⑪ **Let's go to the art exhibition.**
去看藝術展吧！

⑫ **I'd like to rent an audio guide.**
我要租借語音導覽。

⑬ **Do I have to pay for re-entry?**
再進場要付費嗎？

⑭ **Would you like to go mountain climbing with us?**
你想跟我們去爬山嗎？

⑮ **The temperature in the mountain areas is lower.**
山區溫度較低。

⑯ **I'm going camping with my classmates.**
我要和我同學去露營。

⑰ **Who wants to go hiking this weekend?**
這週末誰要去健行？

⑱ **I want to go skiing.**
我想去滑雪。

⑲ **Don't forget your swimsuit and swim cap.**
別忘了帶你的泳裝和泳帽。

⑳ **My folding bike got a flat tire!**
我的小折爆胎了。

㉑ **I'm going to the gym after work. Are you coming along?**
我下班後要去健身房，你要一起來嗎？

原來如此 系列 *E210*

瞬間反應！不用想，立刻講：
馬上開口說英文

打開話匣子，和任何人用英文聊不停！

作　　　者	張瑩安
顧　　　問	曾文旭
社　　　長	王毓芳
編輯統籌	耿文國、黃璽宇
主　　　編	吳靜宜、姜怡安
執行主編	李念茨
執行編輯	陳儀蓁
美術編輯	王桂芳、張嘉容
封面設計	阿作
法律顧問	北辰著作權事務所　蕭雄淋律師、幸秋妙律師

初　　　版	2019年10月
出　　　版	捷徑文化出版事業有限公司
電　　　話	（02）2752-5618
傳　　　真	（02）2752-5619
地　　　址	106 台北市大安區忠孝東路四段250號11樓-1

定　　　價	新台幣320元／港幣107元
產品內容	1書＋MP3

總 經 銷	采舍國際有限公司
地　　　址	235 新北市中和區中山路二段366巷10號3樓
電　　　話	（02）8245-8786
傳　　　真	（02）8245-8718

港澳地區總經銷	和平圖書有限公司
地　　　址	香港柴灣嘉業街12號百樂門大廈17樓
電　　　話	（852）2804-6687
傳　　　真	（852）2804-6409

▶本書部分圖片由Shutterstock提供

捷徑 Book站

現在就上臉書（FACEBOOK）「捷徑BOOK站」並按讚加入粉絲團，
就可享每月不定期新書資訊和粉絲專享小禮物喔！
http://www.facebook.com/royalroadbooks
讀者來函：royalroadbooks@gmail.com

國家圖書館出版品預行編目資料

瞬間反應！不用想，立刻講：馬上開口說英文 /
張瑩安著. -- 初版. -- 臺北市：捷徑文化, 2019.10
　　面；　公分（原來如此：E210）
ISBN 978-957-8904-96-5 (平裝)
1. 英語　2. 會話
805.188　　　　　　　　　　　　　　108014934